THE LIBRARY

N. T. MORLEY

Also by N. T. MORLEY:

The Office
The Castle
The Limousine
The Appointment
The Circle
The Contract
The Parlor

THE LIBRARY

N. T. MORLEY

First Masquerade Edition 1998

ISBN 0-7394-2288-X

Manufactured in the United States of America
Published by Masquerade Books, Inc.
801 Second Avenue
New York, N.Y. 10017

This book is dedicated to Carol Queen,
sexy deviant librarian extraordinaire.

CHAPTER 1

Monique had worked in the library funding office for long enough to have a passing familiarity with the most important donors. But, strangely, she didn't know the name of Pietre Salazar—not until Miss Pynchon said it to her in that moment of accusation, on that most bizarre of all possible Thursdays in September.

Monique would say that name, many times, in her fantasies. She would whisper it over and over again while she touched herself and remembered the stern caresses Pietre had offered her. She would speak his name as a gesture of submission. For Pietre had been her very first, and some special place in the heart is reserved for that.

Most of the time, anyway.

Then again, Monique wasn't really sure. She supposed that Enzo the cleaning guy might have been her very first. Or Hank. Or Phil. Or possibly even Miss Pynchon. It was so difficult to be sure about these things, really.

It depended on how you looked at it.

Submission had figured in Monique's sexual fantasies for years, her sexual release usually being reached while she imagined herself in some exposed and vulnerable position, preferably in front of large numbers of people, being made sexually available against her will. In her fantasies, she would sometimes be taken, but other times she would just be tormented by the knowledge that she was *available* to be taken, unable to resist. She would often climax just thinking of this forced exposure. These fantasies would fill her mind at least several times a day, and usually more than that. Sometimes they would include extended periods of torture or punishment. Monique had endured such fantasies since she had first started to masturbate.

Her fantasies increased in intensity and frequency as she got older. She found her libido growing stronger and stronger, and her fantasies becoming more elaborate and extreme. As the fantasies mounted, Monique found herself wishing she could act them out in real life, wishing she could take on the traits of the ravished slave, unwilling but still unable to resist. Her parents were very wealthy, but instead of finishing college she accepted a job as a clerk in the funding and donations office of a large academic library. Her supervisor, Miss Pynchon, doubtless would have been horrified had she known what was running through her young clerk's mind during the typing of boring memos and fundraising letters.

For Monique's favorite thing about her dull job was that it kept her workdays very quiet and gave her more time to indulge in her fantasies while she was typing memos or performing other menial, repetitive tasks. In fact, it became quite common for Monique to fantasize while she was on the job. And yet she never confessed these fantasies to anyone.

She didn't even describe her longings to the therapist her parents sent her to because she had become so withdrawn and quiet, so acquiescent and meek. Her parents, both rather gregarious types, thought something must certainly be wrong with Monique —why else would she be so quiet? Monique longed to confess her dark fantasies to the therapist, longed to bend herself over the couch in his office and offer herself to him.

But still, Monique had never acted these fantasies out. In fact, Monique never even had sex until she gave herself to Pietre.

It wasn't that Monique was unattractive—on the

contrary, she was quite striking. It could be said that she tended to dress a little "frumpy," since she didn't have the self-confidence to show her body off on a day-to-day basis. But underneath the baggy clothes, Monique's body was smooth and well-proportioned. Though Monique was quite small, just over five feet two, her breasts were large on her frame, and quite firm. Her russet hair showed glorious fair highlights when struck by the light of the sun. Her figure was undeniably enticing, with a slender waist, a flat belly and flared hips, a fine, pert, tight little behind and shapely legs. And her face was the picture of prettiness, both cute and sexy at the same time. Certainly she had full, deep red lips and deep, enchanting green eyes that lowered flirtatiously when she looked at a man. And her sex drive was, without a doubt, in high gear, as if she were a prize desperately waiting to be claimed.

And certainly Monique could have been taken. In fact, there had been several men with whom she had wanted to make love. But they had all come recently. Monique had attended a very conservative girls' high school, so she'd had no chance of meeting boys there. When she was eighteen, she started attending the local community college—much to the horror of her parents, who thought she should have gone to Harvard at least. Though Monique had had good enough grades in high school, her marks in college were less impressive. But even though her grades were nothing special, she was well known with the boys at the community college, and Monique was frequently noticed by them. Many boys, even so, found her intimidating and even a little strange, so while they would comment on her body while Monique's back was turned, they never would have dreamed of asking this strange girl out. After all, she almost never spoke, seemed to have few friends, and seemed to be staring into space most of the time, as if lost in her own thoughts. In the two years Monique had been attending college, only a few boys had been tempted enough to brave the aura of mystery around Monique and ask her out..

Her first boy, Charles, had taken Monique on her very first date ever. Monique tried her best to flirt, but given Monique's intense differences of personality, her flirtation took the form of extreme submission, the desperate attempt to show Charles that she was available to him. She desperately wanted Charles to take her in his arms, undress her, fuck her. She wanted him to make use of all the untapped delights her body had to offer. But Charles had seemed a little frightened of her, as if he didn't understand her. And the best Monique had gotten was a quick peck on the cheek while he was dropping her off. Charles blushed, ran back to his parents Lexus, and drove off, never calling Monique again. He even dropped the class they had together, and Monique felt horrible. She must have done something wrong, she knew. She had committed some great felony against Charles, some horrible transgression of the dating code. She should be punished for it.

But that thought just made Monique more excited, and she got into her bed and masturbated several times with thoughts of Charles punishing her filling her mind.

Knowing that she had somehow offended Charles, Monique sneaked into the human sexuality section of the library in her lunch break, and furtively skimmed as many books on the subject as she could find. She was particularly interested in the self-help books for women on how to be more attractive to men, how to make them crave you all day and all night. But all the books seemed to focus on what to do with a lover *after* he had you in bed. Monique found herself getting quite excited as she read the more explicit sections of the books, especially the ones that described what to do when you went down on a man. Monique decided she would like to do that. She became so excited about it that she had to masturbate, hidden back in a darkened section of the stacks, before returning to work.

From those books, Monique did learn about her clitoris and G-spot, and this knowledge allowed her to increase the frequency of her orgasms by threefold. She became very good at making herself climax, and in fact started to climax before she intended to, especially when she was fantasizing about intensely rough or extreme scenarios. Because of that, she worked on reading the sections about multiple orgasms, and eventually learned to have more than one at a time. This knowledge didn't do much for Monique's "withdrawn" nature. Soon she was having three or more orgasms in a single masturbation session, and her frequency seemed to be increasing as her sex-drive grew. Monique got over the initial discomfort that came with such frequent self-pleasuring, and soon she was accustomed to ten or more orgasms a day. But sometimes she would go two or three days without letting herself come. She imagined it was punishment for some sexual transgression, and her fantasy life was enriched by this thought.

Monique never penetrated herself when she masturbated, much as she longed to. None of the books she'd read were very clear on whether she could hurt herself that way. Clearly the typical woman in one of the dirty books Monique shop-lifted was in intense pain when she was taken for the first time. But Monique couldn't be sure if that happened to every woman when she lost her virginity. Or if she would hurt herself by pressing her finger up inside her sex. Or a cucumber, as she'd fantasized about doing that one time at the family picnic. Either way, Monique knew she wouldn't mind the pain of first penetration one little bit if she was under the weight and warmth of a strong man who owned her completely. But that only made her want to savor it, to keep her virginity for the first man who would have her. And even though Monique's sex was hungry to be filled, she certainly wasn't having any trouble making herself come without fucking herself. She wondered if she would come even harder when a man finally had her?

That thought sent shivers through Monique's body.

The next boy to ask her out was Michael. He had been charming and sexy, and Monique wished desperately that he would make a pass at her. He finally did, toward the end of the evening, and Monique melted into his arms, presenting herself to him. She let him have his way with her, and she desperately wanted to go all the way with him. She was disappointed to find out that "all the way" wasn't very far with Michael. He had her in his arms. He was kissing her deeply, sliding his tongue into her mouth as Monique parted her lips eagerly for him. He had unbuttoned her shirt, was playing with her breasts. The feeling of his strong hands on her breasts was incredible, exciting her to the point where she thought she might climax any second. Michael had taken Monique's hand in his and guided it to the bulge in his pants. Monique had thrilled to close her fingers around its length. She had undone his belt and reached into his pants, and had rubbed eagerly, getting ready to bend down, unzip his pants, and do all the things she had read about—starting by wrapping her lips around his hard cock. Then Michael had groaned as she rubbed, and reached down to press her hand harder against his bulge. Monique felt his warm semen shooting onto her hand, slicking her palm and fingers up. She felt the wetness soaking through his pants. With a shock she realized that he had come already, and he only gave Monique a perfunctory kiss before driving her quickly home. She even had to button up her own shirt. And Michael never asked her out again.

Monique wasn't sure why she had had such lousy luck with men. All the women in the books she speed-read on the back shelf of the bookstore downtown—the one that carried all the books that the library would never, *ever* stock—had their men come into their lives and take them mercilessly, tie them up and do all sorts of wonderful things to them with whips and candle wax. Monique thrilled to read about those, and she even shoplifted the more salacious books, loving them too much to let them go. When she got them home, she felt incredibly guilty about it. Not only was she doing something that she knew was *wrong*—stealing—but she was stealing something so obscene that she would be truly humiliated if she were caught with one of the books stuffed down her skirt. Monique imagined that and became painfully aroused, imagined being forced to strip and being revealed for the slutty little thief that she was. She pictured a roomful of policemen, making her take off all her clothes and discovering porno-graphic paperbacks and nudie magazines stuffed into her bra, her panties, her stockings. She started shoplifting them more often, being careless whenever possible, half-hoping she would be discovered and forcibly strip-searched by a room full of good-looking men in uniform. But she never got caught.

Soon, Monique had a whole complicated network of sexual fantasies, fueled by the cheap paperbacks she read under the covers with a flashlight while getting herself off with her hand. These fantasies involved her being kidnapped by pirates, bikers, thieves; being made the unwilling harem girl of a lusty sultan; being forced into prostitution by drug dealers. There were dozens of other scenarios that formed the basis of Monique's fantasy life. She imagined herself being taken again and again by so many men she lost count.

Monique knew that she was an unusually lusty young woman. She knew this, and she felt some succulent guilt about it. But when the truth was told, Monique had begun to revel in her desires.

CHAPTER 2

Even so, Monique was a virgin when Pietre met her. He was a donor to the library, and Monique met him at one of those cocktail parties for high-level donors. Monique usually didn't get to go to those, but Miss Pynchon, Senior Librarian, Monique's boss and the head of the donor program, had been uncharacteristically kind to Monique and invited her.

Miss Pynchon had never shown much kindness to her single employee, expecting much work and little complaint from the quiet, withdrawn Monique. Miss Pynchon was perhaps thirty-five, and was not by any means an unattractive woman. But her stern manner, her authoritarian posture, her conservative clothes and horn-rimmed glasses, made Monique regard Miss Pynchon as an authority figure and not a friend. Monique always did as Miss Pynchon said, never called in sick and never showed up late. But Miss Pynchon had still never smiled at Monique, and had never offered her a kind word or thanks. Monique didn't mind that she and Miss Pynchon weren't closer; she had come to accept the stern treatment and even to appreciate it—it was more sterile, and allowed Monique to keep more of her own personality hidden. Since so much of her personality involved sexual fantasies of extreme submission, it was much safer this way.

The fundraising party was formal, and Monique knew she would have to dress appropriately. To be totally proper, Monique knew she should bring a date, but she knew *that* was out of the question. In fact, Miss Pynchon had implied, when inviting her, that while the donors and the other employees were welcome to bring a date, Monique was expected to come alone (the implication being that Monique was lucky to be invited at all).

Given the opportunity to go to a formal event for the first time in her life, Monique found herself taking a very uncharacteristic step. The only formal outfit that Monique had was the dress she'd bought for her Senior Ball when she had just turned eighteen. Of course, she hadn't been asked to the ball, and so the dress had never been worn in public. Her mother and father had never even seen the dress on Monique—and that was undoubtedly a good thing. Monique had known that she would not be asked to the ball—despite her fantasies that a strong, dominant boy would invite her at the last minute and take her to the ball naked and on a leash, with her wrists cuffed behind her back, and force her to service all the boys in her class one by one.

There was little chance of that happening, Mon-ique knew. Much as she would have enjoyed it.

But even though she was destined never to wear the dress, she took great pleasure in shopping for one. She enjoyed spending her early graduation gift money from different relatives on *just* the right outfit. The dress she finally bought was a tight, short little thing, and the saleswoman had given Monique a lascivious wink as she'd wrapped it up for her. The blue sequined dress was bare in back, plunging low in front, with a short hem that showed off Monique's stunning legs. Monique had bought elbow-length satin gloves to go with the dress, and a pair of black shoes with four-inch heels, and a pair of black lace-top seamed stockings that affixed to a skimpy lace garter belt. And she also purchased a G-string to go with it. These were the first items of lingerie she'd ever bought, in fact the first underwear with any sort of lace on it that she'd ever owned. She imagined that a man who wanted her on her knees as a slave would expect her to look good in skimpy lace and satin. Of course, with the dress bare in back like that, she couldn't wear a bra. On the night of the Senior Ball, while all her classmates were drinking and dining with abandon, Monique's parents had gone out for dinner and a show. And so Monique stayed at home alone wearing the dress and looking herself over in the mirror, drinking expensive cognac from her parents' liquor cabinet and masturbating furiously. Monique must have come ten times that night, and eventually passed out on the living room, spread out on the floor in front of the big mirror, with the dress hiked up and the G-string pulled out of the way, her legs spread while she rubbed her clitoris furiously.

That had been the only time Monique had worn the dress before the library donors' party. She had been terrified and excited by the prospect of going out in public in that tight little dress. But she got extremely aroused just thinking about it. Of course her parents would never have let her out of the house in such a revealing garment. So Monique had to change in the rest room of the library after work, without going home first. It wasn't until *after* she'd squirmed into the dress that Monique realized that she'd left the G-string at home. She remembered now that she had worn it one day to work, being turned on all day at the thought of the flimsy garment underneath her conservative slacks. But then when she'd tossed the slacks in the laundry, Monique had hidden the G-string under her mattress —the maid would find it if she put it in the laundry, and certainly the maid might tell Monique's parents what she'd found! Monique had never remembered to take that G-string out of its hiding place.

Well, it was too late now. All Monique had were the frumpy white cotton panties—with holes in them, no less—that she usually wore. She put those back on, but it hopelessly ruined the line of the dress, which was much too tight over her firm behind and showed the lines of the panties clearly. That simply wouldn't do!

Then Monique was struck by a wicked idea. She lifted the dress and took the conservative panties off, then smoothed the dress back down and looked at the line of the dress in the mirror. Perfect. The G-string would have worked well too, since it left her pert behind quite bare, but the dress undeniably looked best without anything on underneath it. The idea of going out there with no panties on excited Monique intensely, but she just couldn't imagine herself doing it! Especially not in such a *short* dress. Though Monique was tormented by almost constant exhibitionist fantasies, she never wore a skirt without panties or pantyhose underneath—in fact, she didn't own any skirts that ended above the knee. Now, she was going to go out in front of all those people in this tiny little blue thing, so tight and short, without a single stitch on underneath? She blushed a deep red as she pictured it. But Monique couldn't get the image out of her mind. And there was no way she could wear those panties under this tight dress—they would be visible to everyone.

So Monique wore nothing underneath the dress but her garter belt and stockings. She went out into the part and picked up her name-badge, and started greeting guests as Miss Pynchon had insisted she must.

Knowing how revealed she was, Monique felt her arousal growing with every male guest she greeted. She could feel their eyes on her, taking that tight dress off, roving over every inch of her body. Monique could easily imagine that every one of them knew she wasn't wearing anything underneath. Did they? Could they tell from the way the dress clung to her pretty behind? No, it was impossible. They couldn't know. But God, the way they looked at her—it felt like every one of them was making love to her with his eyes. And the nasty looks she got from women—bitter and unfriendly.

The men, however, plainly approved. And Miss Pynchon seemed the one exception to the rule about women; if anything, she seemed unusually warm to Monique that night. This seemed strange, given Miss Pynchon's usually chilly nature. Perhaps it was just because it was a social occasion.

Monique, though usually so shy, had even found herself learning to flirt a little. The male guests plainly appreciated this, though their wives obviously did not. Monique could feel the warmth growing inside her as she flirted with the men, and as she imagined that they all knew what was—or wasn't—under her dress.

Soon her nipples were quite evident through the

tight material of the dress, and Monique was quite aware that more than a few of the men were paying special attention to them when their eyes roved slowly over her. She was somewhat embarrassed by being so obvious—but she managed to swallow her embarrassment and keep on through the evening as if she hadn't noticed.

Her discomfort was made worse by the fact that her nipples were so exquisitely sensitive. And now, with them so hard, and the material of the dress so tight, they were tingling and aching with every move she made. And it was becoming increasingly harder for Monique to concentrate, or to hide her arousal. Monique was beginning to wish she'd worn panties.

She gulped down glass after glass of white wine— no one had asked whether she was of drinking age, though Miss Pynchon clearly knew that Monique was not. She felt her face flushing, and the heat of the wine didn't do much to lessen her excitement.

Monique was in this state when she first laid eyes on Pietre.

He was considerably older than Monique— perhaps forty—and had an incredible charm to him. He was wearing a tuxedo that looked like it had cost more than the whole library. The way the cut of the tux showed off his firm body was magnificent. Monique hadn't felt a particular attraction to older men just yet—though she had no objection to them—but somehow, this man compelled her. Monique turned part way toward the man, occasionally glancing up at him from across the room, praying that he would come over and talk to her. She had another glass of wine and flushed deeper, feeling suddenly shy. She was about to give up when she saw Pietre looking at her.

But the look wasn't the same as the look the other male patrons were giving her. Their eyes flickered over her from top to bottom, furtively lingering on her breasts, the curve of her hips, the round cheeks of her behind, her legs.

But this man's gaze was riveted to Monique's face —and, particularly, to her eyes. She felt as if his eyes were magnetic, as if he were hypnotizing her. He seemed enraptured, as if he couldn't—or didn't wish to—take his eyes away from Monique's face. She felt a curious warmth running down the length of her body as she stared into his eyes from across the room. She felt as though her knees were going to buckle, as though she was going to fall down on her knees before this man, even in this crowd of people.

Monique felt the heat mounting inside her, as the man continued staring at her. It felt as if his eyes were boring into her, as if he were taking control of her body and her mind. Monique felt flushed, sweat breaking out on her face. She looked away from the man, only to look back a minute later to see he was talking to another partygoer, his gaze finally torn away from Monique. As if he had no reason to look at her body, and as soon as she'd looked away from him he had lost his interest. She quickly gulped another wine, wishing she hadn't looked away. That gaze had been the most erotic thing she had ever felt, the way it flowed through her and warmed her body, enticed her, brought about her intense desire to submit. Monique couldn't concentrate; she was feeling dizzy. She quickly excused herself from the guest she had been chatting with. Monique headed off down the hall to find someplace where she could hide. Her dizziness was getting worse. She slipped into Miss Pynchon's office—which was the closest office that didn't have a glass door.

Monique stumbled across the room and sat down in one of the chairs that faced the desk. She was breathing hard and she felt somewhat ill. The way she felt ill when she became so acutely aroused that she couldn't control herself. She tried to breathe deeply, to slow herself down, but her mind was filled with thoughts of what it would have felt like to drop down to her knees in that roomful of people, to offer herself like that with everyone watching.

Monique lowered her head to her knees, the nervousness making her stomach cramp up. She could smell her own sharp sweat—musk-sweat, the sweat of arousal. Even though she'd been worried earlier that she might have put on too much perfume, her own sexual arousal had defeated the perfume and now filled her nostrils.

Monique was wondering how in hell she was going

to get herself back out there to act as though nothing had happened. She was so sexually excited she wasn't sure she could stop herself from doing something rash. In fact, she was sure she couldn't stop herself. She felt more than a little drunk, but mostly it was the arousal, filling her body and taking control of her mind. Maybe her fantasies had finally gone too far.

That's when Monique heard the door opening.

Damn—she'd forgotten to lock the door.

She hoped it wasn't Miss Pynchon—the frigid bitch got really pissed off if anyone went into her office without permission. Monique turned and looked over her shoulder.

Her breath caught. It was the man from outside, the one who had excited her so.

She turned back around, facing Miss Pynchon's desk, trying not to look at the man.

"I—I'm sorry," she said nervously. "I wasn't feeling well. I...slipped in here to rest for a moment."

"I know," the man said, closing the door behind him. "I followed you."

He locked the door.

The sound of the door-lock clicking sent a bolt of lightning through Monique's body. She sat up straight, fear coursing through her body. What was the man going to do? Was he going to take her against her will? Just the thought of that made sexual desire course through Monique's body.

The man slowly walked up behind Monique, standing close to her. She could feel the warmth of his body. She wondered if he could smell her excitement. Monique closed her eyes.

The man couldn't possibly take her against her will. She would give anything, anything at all, just to be taken by him. Just once. She would lose anything—everything—she had just to give herself to this man she didn't even know.

"My name is Pietre," he said, his voice rich and seductive. He had a faint European accent, though Monique couldn't be sure from where.

"Hi," she said faintly. "I—"

"Not yet," he interrupted. "I don't wish to know your name. Not just yet."

Monique felt his power over her, felt herself surrendering to his energy, his force. She couldn't think straight; her mind was a jumble of conflicting impulses and the pulsing desires of her body.

"You were looking at me out there."

Monique fell silent, her embarrassment causing her face to flush. That's when she felt Pietre reaching down from above her, reaching for the straps of her dress.

"I—I didn't mean to."

"You gave me a look that made me understand what you want. If I've misinterpreted it, please say so."

He edged one strap over Monique's shoulder, then reached for the other.

"But I don't think you will stop me. I think you wanted me to follow you in here."

Monique didn't know if that was true—she'd certainly wanted him, she'd felt the acute desire to throw herself at him. But was he right? Had she known that he would follow her in here?

Maybe she had.

The man pulled the other strap of Monique's dress over her shoulder, began pulling the dress down.

Obediently, Monique uncrossed her arms and let the man pull the dress off her breasts.

"Nothing underneath. Perhaps you were planning for this?"

Monique blushed a still-deeper read, but didn't say anything.

She felt Pietre's hands on her breasts, gently cupping their fullness. She felt him pinching her nipples between thumb and forefinger; she gave a little moan as the pleasure coursed through her body. His touch was electric; her excitement mounted as he pinched her nipples harder.

"Such very nice breasts," he said. "All the men were looking at them out there. Did you notice that?"

Monique felt herself nodding.

"I'm sure you did, you slut. You knew all the men were looking at your breasts. Wanting to put their mouths and hands all over them. Every man in the room wanted these. How delightful that I would be the only one allowed to touch them."

Monique kept her eyes tightly closed, as if that would prevent her from realizing that this was reality—it seemed so much like one of her many fantasies....

"Of course, perhaps you would like to have them touched by every man in the room. Would you like that? If I brought each of the men in here one by one to touch your breasts?"

That sentence hit Monique deep; she felt a new surge of arousal and couldn't suppress a fairly loud moan. The man leaned forward a little, getting his hands more firmly around Monique's breasts and squeezing firmly as he played with the nipples.

"So you *would* like it. They're delightful. What size do you wear? American size, I mean."

Monique hesitated before answering—but not because she questioned Pietre's right to ask her such a personal question. She hesitated because the feeling of Pietre's strong hands on her breasts made it hard for her to find the words.

"Thirty-four C," she whispered nervously.

"Certainly too large for a C," said Pietre.

Monique hesitated again. Then, "A little bit, maybe. Almost. The C is a little tight on me. I...I wear it anyway. I like the way it looks. They're just barely too small for a D. I-I like the way they look in a bra just a little too tight."

"Surely a C must be more than 'a little' too tight. If they're just barely too small for a D."

29

Monique closed her eyes. "Y-yes. The C is more than a little too small. It's quite a bit."

"Uncomfortable sometimes?"

Monique nodded. "But...but I like the way it feels. I like the way they look."

"But you're not wearing anything on them right now. Nothing at all. Did you know you were going to make such a slut of yourself tonight?"

Monique moaned again, unable to find the words to answer him.

The man bent low, putting his mouth to Mon-ique's ear so she could feel his warm breath. He pinched his nipples harder and rolled them in his fingers. Monique fought to keep her thighs slightly spread; the excite-ment was coursing through her, and the stimulation of having her nipples played with was almost too much. She could almost come like this. If she he touched her pussy at all, Monique knew she probably would come before much longer.

The man said: "I asked you if you knew you were going to be a slut tonight. Such a slut."

"N-no," gasped Monique.

"Surely you knew your nipples were visible to every-one? That every man in the room was undressing you? And probably most of the women, too. You knew that, didn't you?"

Monique shuddered slightly, then whispered, "Yes."

"Both the men and the women. Taking your clothes

off. Imagining what you would feel like against them. Did you like that?"

Monique couldn't stop herself. She told the truth.

"Yes," she breathed.

"The women, too? Do you like women? In that way, I mean—the way you like men. To go to bed with them?"

Monique's pussy quivered. She hadn't thought about it like that—not really. But she had certainly noticed that a few of the women were looking at her with gazes at least as lustful as the men's.

"Do you like women? Do you like to make love with girls as well as boys?"

Monique nodded quickly. "Yes," she sighed.

Pietre chuckled. His hands left her breasts, though he still stood very close behind her.

"Stand up, my dear," he said.

Monique didn't even think about disobeying. Somehow, without meaning to do so, she had come under this incredible man's power. Now she obeyed his every whim, and Monique knew she could not deny him. What was happening to her?

Monique stood up, and the man's hand came to rest on the small of her back. He pushed her forward slightly, and Monique stumbled a little and caught herself against the edge of Miss Pynchon's desk. She didn't realize until that moment that she had instinctively kept her legs apart perhaps two feet.

She wanted to close him, but she felt like she

couldn't. Not until the man gave her an order to do so.

The man kicked the chair out of the way, came up behind Monique. Monique felt the hardness of his body against her. He quickly took hold of the hem of her dress and pulled it up, swiftly, to her waist, exposing her naked behind and her dripping sex.

"Nothing on under here, either," said the man with some pleasure. "Surely you knew you were going to make a slut of yourself."

"Yes," whispered Monique. She was beyond caring; she only wanted this man to take her, to spread her out on Miss Pynchon's desk and take her mercilessly, fucking her over and over and over again—

"Then you must be wet," said the man. "I imagine your sex is so very wet down there." His way of speaking seemed exotic, unusual—English clearly wasn't his first language. But the strange way he spoke excited Monique that much more.

Monique felt acutely humiliated, but she couldn't deny it. She couldn't deny him anything.

"Yes," she said softly. "I'm very wet."

"Are you sure?" He said mischievously.

Monique quickly nodded her head.

"Why don't you reach down and make certain?" asked Pietre.

Monique's head was spinning. She couldn't be doing this with a stranger—not here, at work, against Miss Pynchon's desk, with a man she'd never met or even seen before tonight, a man who didn't even know her name—and didn't want to!

But she was. She was doing it.

She took one hand off Miss Pynchon's desk, steadied herself with the other hand, leaning forward as she reached down to touch her sex. She slipped one finger up and down the length of her slit, feeling how wet it was. God, she was dripping. She stroked herself up and down, teasing her clit, feeling the intense sensations, mounting toward orgasm. She realized that she was moaning softly.

"Well?"

"Yes," panted Monique. "I'm wet. I'm very wet."

The man pressed up against her, his bulge against her ass. It felt enormous. His arms curved around Monique and he began to play with her breasts again. Monique's moans increased; the man began to kiss the back of her neck, another of Monique's most sensitive spots.

"Then reach back," he said. "Go on. Find what's waiting for you."

Monique's hand left her sex eagerly, and she reached behind her to spread her fingers around the bulge in his pants. God, it felt enormous. Monique tried to unfasten the tuxedo pants; she fumbled hopelessly.

"Come," said the man after Monique had tried in vain to undo his pants. "You must have done this before."

Monique's eyes filled with tears and her hand froze, still pressed against the bulge of his cock. She shook her head, "No."

There was a long silence as Monique's fingers tightened around the man's bulge.

Pietre chuckled. "Of course you mean not with a man in tuxedo pants?"

A single sob wracked Monique's body, and she shook her head fervently.

"I mean... never," she whispered. "I've never done it. Never made love. Never had sex. Never."

"Never been fucked?"

Monique nodded. "Never been fucked," she breathed.

Another long silence, as Monique felt sure the man was deciding to reject her, to leave without sampling her.

Then, to Monique's surprise, he chuckled.

"A virgin? You mean to say...you're a virgin?"

Monique nodded sadly, another sob spasming through her body.

The man chuckled again, pulled away from Monique. Monique slumped against Miss Pynchon's desk, her arousal swirling together with her madness.

The man produced a card from his pocket. Monique felt him slipping it into the rumpled back of her dress, where the hem was pulled up to her waistline, exposing her curved behind.

"I think this Wednesday, at one in the afternoon,

would be an appropriate time. Guard that maidenhead of yours until then, you little slut. Whatever your name is."

Monique heard his footsteps, then the door opening and then closing behind him. She leaned against the desk, overcome with her own painful arousal, but knowing that she could not possibly get herself off in Miss Pynchon's office. Monique found herself sobbing, not in sadness or humiliation, but because she'd been so close, and had not been taken. She felt as though her whole body was on fire. She could smell the sweetness of her sex, the telltale sign that her body was ready for sex. But again she'd been denied.

She picked up the card and looked at it. It said only "Master Pietre," then gave an address and phone in an upscale neighborhood very close to where Monique's parents lived. In fact, it was walking distance.

With shaking, nervous hands, Monique pulled her dress back on, then tucked the card into her dress—the dress had no pockets, so the only place to hide it was in her cleavage, which felt vaguely naughty. She went out to the party again. Telling Miss Pynchon she wasn't feeling well, Monique caught a ride home with some library donors who lived near her parents, and went quickly up to her room.

That night, she masturbated so fervently and so many times that she was afraid her parents might have heard the bed thrashing back and forth, and her cries of orgasm, which she tried unsuccessfully to muffle with her pillow. The climaxes were so hard and sudden that night that she couldn't stop herself from making noise. By the time she finally slept it was after one in the morning, and she woke up three more times through the night with the ache in her body, fantasies of the dark stranger, Pietre, filling her mind. She woke up hung over and with an intense ache in her sex from over-stimulation. She managed to make it to work only a half-hour late, for which she received a bit of a dressing-down from Miss Pynchon. Monique couldn't help but imagine the dressing-down she would have gotten if Miss Pynchon had known what had transpired the previous night.

Monique spent the week in a state of frenzied sexual desire. She tried to hide her constant arousal, but it was hard to do. She found herself anticipating Thursday with a curious terror and delight. Monique hoped she would be allowed to give herself to Pietre—and wondered what that would look like. Would it resemble her fantasies? What things would be expected of her as she knelt before her man?

On Wednesday, Monique nervously blurted out to Miss Pynchon that she had a doctor's appointment the next day. It wasn't until after she'd said it that Monique realized how foolish that was. After all, she had no idea how long she would be...indisposed...with Pietre.

Would he take her as a lover? Certainly, then, she should make herself available to him all afternoon. But Miss Pynchon was unwilling to give Monique the afternoon off. Monique toyed with the idea of calling the phone number on the card and asking Pietre if she could come another time. But that thought only lasted a moment; Monique knew that she could not possibly question Pietre's orders. Rather, it excited her to strive to follow his demands, to meet him at the appointed time, even though Miss Pynchon was most unpleasant about it. She detested it when her employees had appointments during the day. Finally, Monique said she would be back at three. Two hours? Would that be enough time?

Monique felt somewhat nasty, like a whore making an appointment with a trick. She supposed that was fairly close to the truth....

Monique's spare moments were filled with frenzied masturbation, desperate wanking locked away in her bedroom or in the employee ladies' room at the library. It seemed that she couldn't be alone without wanting to slip her hand between her legs and stroke her sex, to feel its delicate wetness, touch its fragility and think about the moment when Pietre took her. She could almost feel him penetrating her, could almost feel his weight upon her body. She could picture him mounting her, taking her. Monique had read through all the self-help books in the library and knew the wide variety of positions in which a man could take a woman. How would Pietre do it? Would he take her from behind the first time? With Monique on her hands and knees, ass in the air? Or bent over an armchair with her legs spread wide? Or would he prefer to do it slowly, languidly, with Monique on her back, spread wide for him, sex exposed for him to take her in the missionary position?

Surely it wouldn't be this last one, for the sex books made it sound like nobody at all was doing it that way any longer. Not these days.

Perhaps he would want Monique to be on top, doing the work. Monique found it more intensely arousing to think about the positions with Pietre on top of her, since her entire body was filled with the desire to submit to him. But Monique could imagine her lover making her give herself in this way, so that she was more active in her own deflowerment. In a way, that was even me submissive, demanding that Monique climb on top of her lover and push it in, breaking her own maidenhead. God, the very thought made Monique wet to the knees.

Or perhaps Pietre would take her standing up, as she'd been the night in Miss Pynchon's office when he'd almost fucked her. Monique cursed herself whenever she thought of that. If she hadn't hesitated like that, hadn't told Pietre that she was a virgin...he would have entered her right then, and she would have lost her virginity leaning against Miss Pynchon's desk. She had been so ready for it she couldn't imagine it hadn't happened that night.

But she felt sure it would happen on Thursday. Monique felt more than a little strange about scheduling her deflowerment like this. But even so, every thought of her "appointment" with Pietre drove her mad with arousal.

Monique usually drove a little red sports car her parents had bought her for her sixteenth birthday. But the car was in the shop that day, so she had to take the bus from downtown, and even had to walk past her parents house to get to the address Pietre had given her. Her parents were both at work, but the maid, Mariette, was probably home, and Monique felt a little nervous about the thought that the maid might see her walking by. Even though Mariette was only nineteen, a domestic from France, she seemed to take great pleasure in telling on Monique. Monique was sure that if Mariette saw her walking by the house in the middle of the day, it would get back to her parents and she'd have to make up some plausible story. But even so, Monique found that she didn't want to change her route to go around the house. Rather, the thought that she might get caught excited her. It added to the arousal she felt walking to keep her appointment with destiny.

It was a hot afternoon. Monique had struggled that

morning with what she should wear. Her fantasy was to wear the evening dress, as unadorned as it had been that night at the library. But that wasn't possible, since she was on foot. So she had worn a black knit pencil skirt, one that came to her knees. But just before she left the library, Monique had ducked into the ladies' room and had doubled the skirt up, pinning it with a safety pin so it only came to mid-thigh. It just wouldn't do to keep an appointment like this wearing a skirt of such a length.

Monique had also seen to the other parts of her outfit, slipping off her panties and bra so that she wore nothing at all under the skirt and sweater. This made her feel deliciously exposed and vulnerable. Since Monique was wearing an extremely tight sweater—one three sizes too small that she hadn't worn in years, but had kept in the closet with this sort of occasion wickedly in mind—her breasts were quite evident. Especially since the anticipation had made her nipples rock-hard.

Monique was wearing a pair of black shoes she'd bought in a thrift store—three-inch heels, not quite as slutty as the pair she'd been wearing the night she'd met Pietre, but more daring than usual for her. In fact, with the skirt pinned up and the tight sweater on, those heels did make Monique look more than a little slutty.

To Monique's embarrassment, Miss Pynchon had seen her coming out of the ladies' room, and had looked very shocked when she saw Monique's outfit.

"Ready for your doctor's appointment, Monique?" she asked sarcastically.

Monique pretended not to hear Miss Pynchon. Blushing, she rushed down the hall before Miss Pynchon could ask more embarrassing questions. But Monique knew that she was in for it when she got back—she would be interrogated as to why, exactly, she had felt the need to dress like a slut to go to her doctor's appointment.

Miss Pynchon would probably already know the answer. And Monique would be in trouble.

But she didn't want to have that discussion yet. Not until after she'd kept her appointment with Pietre. Nothing was more important than that.

It was a hot day, and walking to Pietre's house left her soaked in sweat and feeling sticky. She could feel the sweat dripping down her thighs... or perhaps that was something else.

She found the address Pietre had given her. It was a stunning mansion with marble pillars in front and a huge turnabout that could hold at least ten cars; there were a Jaguar, a Maseratti and a Rolls Royce parked there now, but off to one side was a large garage that must have sheltered still more cars. There was a fountain in the front yard, and the entry was protected by an iron gate. But the gate had been left open.

Monique walked up to the front door and reached

up to knock the magnificently ornate knocker. She hesitated, her fear overwhelming her for a moment. What was she doing? She was about to throw herself at a stranger, to give herself to someone who didn't even know her name.

Then a shudder went through her body, and she tried to shore up her inner strength. She was going to need it. This was everything she'd ever wanted. Something in the way Pietre had looked at her, commanded her with his eyes. Something made her want him, want to belong to him.

Monique reached up, lifted the brass knocker, and brought it down firmly with a hollow knock.

Chapter 3

Monique waited for what seemed like several minutes. She stood in the uncomfortable heat, nervous and fidgeting. Finally, the door creaked open slowly. There stood a man in a tuxedo, perhaps a bit older than Pietre, wearing white gloves. He was dressed like a butler or servant.

The butler's eyes roved over Monique's tight-fitting sweater, lingering on her breasts. He regarded her body with open lust but an equally obvious expression of disdain, of contempt. Monique felt herself withering under the man's gaze; even though he seemed like a servant, there was something a little frightening about him. Almost as though he possessed the same kind of power that Pietre did. Or was it that Monique was more sensitive to the dominance of males now that her sexual self had been awakened by this curious encounter?

She couldn't be sure.

"Pietre sent for me," Monique finally blurted when perhaps half a minute of uncomfortable silence had passed.

"I'm well aware that the Master is expecting a visitor," said the butler. "He's quite ready for you. You're almost four minutes late." The contempt in the butler's expression grew stronger as his eyes lingered, this time even more forcefully, on Mon-ique's large breasts. She shivered despite the heat, felt herself squirming under the man's gaze. She felt as though she was being forcibly undressed, exposed before him. And he was making no attempt to disguise his appreciation of her features, or his contempt for her. But rather than feeling angry or threatened, Monique felt her resolve melting, felt herself longing to turn that obvious contempt into desire.

"I-I'm sorry," muttered Monique quickly. "I'm... I'm very sorry. I didn't realize how long the bus would take."

"Not to worry," said the butler. "Do come in."

He held the door for Monique. She walked into the ice-cold mansion and immediately felt a chill go down her spine. It was quite a contrast to the heat outside. Monique felt her nipples stiffening in the sudden cold.

The entryway was incredible, expansive and open,

with marble floors and rich Oriental rugs, carved wooden chairs and what looked like Renaissance paintings on the walls. All the paintings showed nude women, often in somewhat sexually suggestive positions—more suggestive than the Renaissance would have allowed, so Monique didn't think they could be that old. But there was something more. The women all seemed to be in vaguely...submissive poses. The expressions on their faces mixed sexual availability with an obvious eagerness to obey.

Monique shivered.

The butler asked: "May I get you something? Something to drink?"

The butler's eyes lingered again over Monique's breasts, focusing, in particular, on the erect buds of her nipples, quite visible under the tight sweater. Monique shifted nervously, feeling herself once again stripped by the man's gaze.

Monique nervously muttered, "Perhaps a red wine," trying to sound as sophisticated as possible.

"Merlot or Cabernet?"

Meekly, Monique said, "either."

The man's sneer of contempt made Monique feel even more exposed and vulnerable. This guy was obviously a snob, but even so she felt somehow that she was deeply inadequate and should make amends. That feeling started to warm her against the formidable cold of the mansion.

"I'll show you to the parlor," he said, walking down a long, richly carpeted hallway. "The Master will meet you there." The butler led Monique into a lavishly furnished sitting room with mounds of soft red cushions on two facing loveseats and several divans. There were paintings on these walls, too, four or five of them, but Monique saw as she looked around at them that these were slightly more explicit than the ones in the entryway. The difference might not have been so obvious to someone who didn't share Monique's predilections. But it was clear: the women in these paintings were in positions of distress or submission. One woman was on her knees in a pose that might just have had her picking flowers...or perhaps it meant something more. Another painting showed a nude woman on a horse, looking very helpless, menaced by wild beasts. Still another had a naked woman bound to the bow of a sailing ship in the midst of a storm.

"Please make yourself quite comfortable," said the butler with a smirk. "I will bring you the wine."

Monique sat down uncomfortably on one of the loveseats, and found herself sinking into the rich satin cushions; her legs flew up and she struggled to get back into a sitting position. She kept her thighs pressed tightly together, acutely aware of the fact that she wasn't wearing anything under the skirt. Nervously, Monique sat on the very edge of the soft couch, knowing full well that if she leaned back she might be lost in all that softness. It had been deliciously comfortable, though. It would be so pleasant simply to sink into the couch and have a nap, not to worry about whether she was doing something incredibly stupid...

And why not? Monique was aware almost for the first time that she had come here to keep an appointment with a lover, and that she would probably make love for the first time in this house, would probably give herself to a man as she had never done before.

Thinking about this, Monique let herself slide back into the softness of the satin-covered couch, feeling its caress all over her body. Monique sank back until she was almost lost in the comfort. She worked to keep her thighs together, but she could feel the skirt riding up as she squirmed. She felt suddenly very tired.

She looked up helplessly at the paintings on the walls. Just looking at them excited her; did Pietre know what kind of fantasies she had? Had he somehow sensed it in Monique—was that why he had followed her into the office and given her his card?

Or was it simply a coincidence that the women in these paintings were in positions that Monique longed to assume? Situations that she fantasized about?

It couldn't be a coincidence, could it?

The butler returned carrying a tray with a bottle of red wine and one glass. Monique struggled to get into a sitting position again, well aware as she did so that her skirt had ridden up quite far on her thighs. If she were to let her thighs slip apart, she would be giving the butler an unforgivable and obvious beaver shot. God, she couldn't do that.

Finally, a very deeply blushing Monique was sitting up straight on the edge of the couch. She quickly moved over to the divan, which afforded more stable seating. The butler lifted one eyebrow and looked down at Monique somewhat contemptuously as he popped the cork on the wine.

He poured the wine, and Monique accepted the glass.

"The Master will be in to see you," he said, and closed the door behind him as he left.

Monique felt a jolt of electricity going through her as she heard him turning the latch on the other side—that had to be a key.

Monique got up and went to the door. She bent down to look through the old-fashioned keyhole and saw that the key had been taken out of the lock. Monique felt a rising excitement as she realized that she'd been locked in. She couldn't leave now if she wanted to.

She felt sure that she ought to be upset and terrified by that fact, but she couldn't stop the powerful tingling it aroused in her loins. She tested the door and found it heavy, secure, immobile. She walked around the room to each of the windows—and discovered that none of them opened. They didn't match the door—they weren't the old-fashioned type. They were a more modern type of window of the sort you might see in a hotel. They couldn't open at all, and as Monique tapped on the windowpane she was surprised at how thick and unbreakable the glass felt. It almost seemed like safety glass. And what's more, the decorative patterns in the windowpane, she realized, were made of metal filigree, which meant that even if she were able to break the window, which she probably couldn't, she wouldn't be able to climb through.

Monique felt a sense of panic rising in her body. She should be terrified, shouldn't she? Something was very wrong with this. She had come here to keep an appointment with the man she thought would be her first lover. And now it seemed that he was taking her prisoner.

Monique laughed a little at herself. She was being silly. Certainly she wasn't Pietre's prisoner. He was just playing a little game with her. He was teasing her.

Then the panic returned, and Monique realized that if Pietre wasn't teasing her—if he really intended to take her prisoner, then there wasn't a thing she could do about it. The parlor was quite secure—there was no way out. She went around to each of the windows again, testing them, knocking on them, desperately looking for a way out—just so she would know there was one. But she had no luck—she was trapped. She tested the door once again, and found it just as solid as before. There was no way out.

Monique's sense of fear increased as she realized what an effect her unexpected imprisonment was having on her. She was achingly aroused, her sex moist with excitement. Her nipples were quite painfully erect, not from the cold—for this room was quite a bit warmer than the entryway, and Monique was becoming uncomfortably hot because of her own internal fires. But the terror was taking precedence right now, which only served to mount her pleasure higher. Monique felt as though she was spinning out of control.

She sat down on the divan and gulped some of the red wine. It was incredibly good, and she saw from the label that it was a thirty-year-old vintage. Monique poured another glass with shaking hands, and when she'd gulped down that one, she poured another.

She felt an intense fear at the knowledge that she was completely trapped. She was Pietre's prisoner here, if she hadn't been already. After all, wasn't she captivated from the moment she saw him at the party? From the moment she saw him looking at her like that, taking possession of her with her eyes? Hadn't she come here hoping to become his lover—but more than that? Not simply his lover, but his servant. His property.

Monique could feel the warmth of the alcohol working its way up her body, filling her with a curious relaxation. Every cell of her body vibrated with the knowledge that she had been imprisoned, that she was already under Pietre's power. That knowledge, along with the excellent red wine, began to work its magic upon her body. She could feel the desire rising inside her. Soon Monique had relaxed into the softness of the big couch, feeling herself on all sides by its plush red velvet. She let her legs drift apart, acutely aware that the skirt was riding up on her thighs, which left her sex vividly exposed for Pietre's eyes if he happened to walk through the door. Or the butler's eyes, for that matter. Monique rubbed her body against the satin of the sofa and the pillows, feeling the sensuous delights all around her body.

His prisoner, she repeated in her mind over and over again. *I am his prisoner. I am Pietre's prisoner. He has had me imprisoned. Against my will. And yet I came willingly. I presented myself to him.* Monique found her hand straying up the inside of her splayed thighs, stroking the soft flesh there. Then her hand was on her sex, and the other hand slid up inside her tight sweater, cupping one of her breasts and playing with the nipple. Then she was pinching the nipple hard, rolling it between thumb and forefinger, while she stroked her exposed sex eagerly. Monique whimpered and moaned uncontrollably, her body thrashing back and forth on the soft couch. She reached up just long enough to pull the skirt off; then her hand returned to her sex. She would have taken the sweater off; she was getting uncomfortably hot squirming around like this. But no, she couldn't do that...she couldn't strip totally naked on the couch like that. That would be so awful of her. *As delicious as it would be just to slip this sweater off and be naked for him. For Pietre.* But the real reason she couldn't take her hands off her sex or her breast; her desire was rising incredibly fast and she desperately wanted to get herself off.

I can't believe I'm doing this, she repeated over and over again in her head while she stroked herself and moaned. *I can't be doing this. Not spread out on the couch like this, with my skirt off, my legs spread. What if Pietre comes in? He'll think I'm the perfect slut. A complete trollop, who can be had by anyone. But he already thinks that of me. He already thinks I'm a desperate little virgin who can't wait to get her cherry popped. That I'm dying to go to bed with him. Why else would I have acted like that in Miss Pynchon's office? He knew what I wanted from the moment he saw me at the party. Now he's brought me here to make me humiliate myself. he's going to find me like this, half-stripped, wanking on his couch. He's going to find me, going to see what a slut I am. His prisoner. I'm his prisoner. He has imprisoned me....*

Monique's pleasure mounted as she rubbed herself, as she stroked her breasts. Almost without knowing she was doing it, she got the sweater off and it disappeared into the cushions of the couch. She was now stark naked, helplessly jilling off on the couch. Her moans grew louder, now that she'd completely revealed herself to be the slut she was. Monique began to work her hips up and down in time with her hands as she closed in on her orgasm. She breathed faster and faster as she neared her pinnacle. She arched her back, throwing her head from side to side as the familiar sensation of impending orgasm filled her. But Monique was tottering on the edge as she realized that a key was scraping in the lock. How could she not have heard that earlier? Fear gripping her, Monique gasped and sat up, groping desperately for her clothes. Then she froze in that position—perhaps it was Pietre, about to enter the room to fuck her. To take her. Monique slipped her hand back between her legs and began rubbing her pussy again, feeling how close to orgasm she was. She was still doing that when the door opened and the butler came in.

Monique's face flushed hot. She started searching desperately for her clothes. Monique got her sweater, but couldn't find the skirt. She glanced around furtively for the skirt as she looked up at the butler, her face turning deep red with humiliation.

The butler looked shocked; his eyes flickered up and down Monique's revealed body as she crossed her legs tightly and tried to hold the sweater in front of her, hiding her breasts from him. But the butler's gaze seemed to burn right through her, and she knew damn well that he knew exactly what she'd been doing.

Finally, Monique stopped searching for the skirt and just sat there looking dumbly at the butler. After what felt like hours of silence, the butler spoke to Monique coldly.

"The Master is unable to meet with you today," he said. "He sends his regrets. I am to escort you out."

Monique's whole body seemed ripe and desperately hungry for orgasm, ready to be fucked. Monique was so overwhelmed with desire that the thought even occurred to her of throwing herself at the butler. But that wouldn't be possible—she just couldn't do such a thing! Even so, the ache filling her body made her embarrassment much worse. Monique felt her face flushing even deeper, humiliation overwhelming her. She felt tears welling in her eyes. She had blown it. Pietre had somehow seen what she was doing—perhaps he peeked through the keyhole while she was wanking—and it had offended him—as Monique should have known it would! How could she have done such a thing? It was so com-pletely absurd, to be invited over to a man's house and then to just strip naked like a complete hussy. Monique couldn't believe she'd done it.

"I am to escort you out," the butler repeated coldly, still staring at Monique. From his posture he made it quite obvious that he did not intend to leave the room or avert his gaze.

Monique blurted, "Will he see me again...another time?"

"I am to escort you out," the butler repeated, his tone making it very clear that this was the *last* time he intended to repeat that particular phrase.

Monique wanted to ask him to turn around or leave the room, to give her some privacy in putting her clothes back on. But she shouldn't have had them off in the first place, and she was too embarrassed to ask the butler for anything at that moment. So she shyly turned to one side while she struggled in to the tight sweater, aware the whole time that the butler was watching her every move, inspecting every curve of her available body. Then Monique hunted around for the skirt, contorting her body into awkward positions trying to keep her lower body out of the butler's line of sight. She finally slipped off the edge of the couch and fell to one knee in front of it, aware that the angle she was at now gave the butler a perfect view of her behind and probably even let him see her sex between her legs. Feeling acutely humiliated, Monique groped for the skirt while the butler looked her over. She finally found the skirt wedged under the couch cushion—how had it gotten there—and she quickly squirmed into it, still trying to position her body so that the butler would see as little of her as possible. When she finally stood, smoothing down the sweater and the skirt over her, she realized that her nipples, still hard from arousal and from being played with, were quite evident through the sweater. That had seemed like such a good idea earlier in the day, wearing a tight sweater like that. But now it seemed so ridiculous, and Monique felt so intensely embarrassed as she saw the butler looking at her disdainfully. Without a word, the butler turned and began to lead Monique to the door.

Monique followed behind meekly, dejected. She was convinced that she'd spoiled her chance, that she'd lost Pietre's interest. She felt as though she was about to burst out in tears. She fought back her embarrassment as she was led to the door.

At the door, she paused a moment and turned back and said desperately, "Can you have him call me?"

The butler said only, "My instructions are that I am to see you out." With that, he closed the door, and Monique was left on the doorstep on the brink of tears.

CHAPTER 4

Monique felt tears welling up in her eyes as she waited
for the bus. She tried to hold back her sobs, but she
succumbed to them for a few minutes while waiting
there. How could she have blown it like this with
Pietre? He had seemed so interested in her, so ready to
give her what she so desperately wanted. And she had
been so willing to give it up for him. Monique was
crushed. She was so crushed, in fact, that she entirely
forgot what she was wearing. Before leaving work, she
had changed into clothes that were correct for a slut,
the slut she wanted to be. She had pinned up her skirt
so that it revealed her shapely legs, and put on the
sweater that was several sizes too small. If she hadn't

been crying while she stood at the bus stop, she would doubtless have noticed the hungry glances of men driving or walking by, the catcalls from passing cars, the whistles and howls from teenage boys passing on their way to after-school hangouts. But as it was, Monique was oblivious to the attention she was receiving, thinking only of what a failure she'd been in seducing Pietre. She had been sure he wanted her! And oh, how she'd wanted him!

The bus was a long time coming, having doubtless been delayed by early homeward-bound traffic. It was almost three by the time the bus stopped and Monique boarded. That meant she'd be late getting back to the library. Miss Pynchon probably already knew that Monique hadn't really gone to the doctor. Monique wondered what her punishment might be, or whether Miss Pynchon would even confront her on it at all.

As she stepped onto the bus and paid her fare, Monique realized what she was wearing, realized how exposed she still was. The bus driver looked her up and down appreciatively and let his eyes linger on her full, shapely breasts and her pretty face. Monique felt an acute sense of embarrassment—the bus driver probably thought she was some sort of whore.

Then Monique looked into the bus and saw that it was rather full. It was getting closer to rush hour, and the bus was now quite full with commuters. With some dismay, Monique realized that the bus riders were almost all men. This meant that Monique's smooth legs and full breasts were displayed quite plainly for more men than Monique had ever shown off for like this.

In fact, Monique felt their hot glances undressing her, touching her all over as she stood at the front of the bus. But that wasn't the only thing that made Monique suddenly uncomfortable. Standing there, she realized that her pussy, so wet from her arousal at Pietre's house, was gently drizzling down her inner thighs, unencumbered by panties or a slip. She had to press her thighs together to stop the steady dripping of her sexual fluids. And her nipples, which were already hard, felt even harder in the appreciative gazes of the bus driver and the men riding the bus.

But the worst thing of all was that there were no seats left on the bus. Surely one of the men could have offered Monique a seat, but they did not. They probably all thought they could get a better view of her if she was forced to stand. Monique took hold of the overhead bar just as the driver gunned the engine violently; the bus jerked and Monique almost fell, causing her to press against another of the standing commuters. She could feel his crotch pressing against her through the tight skirt, the sensation made more noticeable by the fact that Monique was not wearing anything under the skirt. Monique felt the man's hand on her waist, helping her back into a standing position. Her face turned a deeper red and she tried not to look back at the guy.

That momentary contact had seemed electric, since it was punctuating an already extreme sexual excitement Monique felt from being looked at like this by all the men on the bus.

Monique stood there feeling the men look her over, feeling her shame. But why should she feel ashamed? The men were consumed with wanting her, were admiring her attributes; the excitement she felt was a natural reaction. But still, Monique felt that she was displaying herself in a shameful manner. Even so, she couldn't stop the feeling of arousal that was overwhelming her as she stood there with her hands over her head.

I must present a pretty picture, she thought. *On display like this. My hands over my head. Like they're bound there. Tied with rope. Or chained. Manacled over my head. I'm chained here. All these men are undressing me with their eyes. Undressing me. Stripping me. I can feel them on me. Lifting up my sweater. I'm not wearing anything underneath. Exposing my breasts. I'm manacled with my hands over my head. I'm chained to this bar. I can't resist them. I can't stop them from stripping me. They're pulling off my skirt. Making me step out of it. Now I'm naked in front of all of them. All of them. They're all looking at me, naked.*

The bus stopped, and a large number of people got on. This meant that Monique was jostled back further into the bowels of the bus. She felt warm bodies, all of them male, pressing in around her. Then pressing against her. She felt herself enclosed by their heat.

They're pressing in all around me. Surrounding me. Holding me chained here. Running their hands all over me.

As the commuters fought to get a place on the bush, those in the back—Monique included—were crammed uncomfortably against each other. Monique was forced out away from the standee pole, and had to reach for a handhold in the center of the aisle, directly over her head. The handhold was a leather strap, fastened to the ceiling. It was obviously made for someone quite a bit taller than Monique's modest five-foot-two, and she had to stand on her tiptoes to hold the strap. That only made her more unstable, which forced her to lean against the man behind her. Monique was about to readjust herself to try to pull away, but then she felt something that made her stop.

Monique's barely covered ass was pressed back against the man's crotch. More importantly, she was on her tiptoes, so her ass leaning back against him was providing an important point of support for Monique. She was shocked at how good it felt to have her buttocks pressed against this man's body, against this stranger's crotch. But what made Mon-ique stop moving was this: the guy felt hard. At first Monique thought it was just his belt. But then she decided that couldn't be it. What's worse, he seemed to be getting harder as

Monique unwillingly wriggled her ass against him. The bus ride was quite rough, and Monique had to squirm a little just to hang on and stand upright. Since she was on her tiptoes already, Monique couldn't do a thing to stop the jostling motions of her ass against him. Well, maybe she could have found something...but Monique found, to her shock, that she didn't want to.

Monique slipped her wrist through the strap over her, let it hold her firmly. She could feel the leather biting into her wrist—it felt just like a strap. Just like a leather restraint, fastening her to the ceiling. *I'm padlocked here*, Monique thought to herself. *I'm locked here with my hands over my head, tied up, and I'm naked. Totally naked in front of all these men. They've stripped me bare. Now this man has come up behind me to fuck me. He's going to take me. He knows I'm a virgin, and he's going to be extra-rough because of it. He's holding onto me, getting ready to force it into me.*

Monique's mind was racing, her body flushed with the heat of the bus. Her fantasy was making her so turned on that she could feel the moisture drizzling down her inner thighs. *Oh God*, she thought, *I wish I'd worn panties...I'm dripping on the floor...I'm so incredibly wet....*

Monique turned briefly to look at the guy. His face was bright red; he looked incredibly embarrassed. But despite that, he was pretty cute, mid-thirties with a nice smile. Monique turned back around and tried to close her mind off from thinking about him, thinking about how good he felt pressing against her like that. Hard and ready to take her.

Monique couldn't stop her mind from racing like that. With every jiggle of the bus, she felt her ass pressing against the bulge in the man's crotch, felt the skirt riding up. If she didn't do something soon, it was going to ride up over the curve of her ass and anyone who looked down would see that Monique wasn't wearing any panties.

But Monique didn't move to do anything—not just yet.

Instead, she snuggled her ass more firmly against the guy's crotch. Now she could feel the outline of his cock most distinctly, could feel its length pressing up between her cheeks. And Monique's mind was running wild with the possibilities of the situation.

I wonder if this guy knows he could just lift my skirt a few inches and fuck me. I wonder if he knows I would let him do it. If he knows I want him to do it. I want him to take my skirt and pull it up and just fuck me right here on the bus with everyone watching... and then all of them, too, since I'm chained here and I can't move or resist them.... I'm forced to stand here and take their cocks...one after the other....

Monique was almost delirious with her hunger. She was going to do it. She was going to reach back and take hold of the guy's cock and get it out of his pants and push herself back onto it. She was going to lose her virginity on this crowded bus with all these men watching and cheering as she was deflowered...

Suddenly getting flustered, Monique nervously pulled her skirt down and leaned forward ever so slightly, taking the pressure off of the guy's hard-on, breaking the contact between her flesh and his in that crucial juncture. The guy behind her breathed a sigh of relief, and Monique felt relieved that she hadn't actually fucked the guy. She was about ready to.

But now she could feel her breasts pressing against the back of the guy in front of her. With the way her nipples felt, she was sure the guy must have been able to feel them, too. He must have been able to feel the hardness of her nipples on his back as Monique jiggled back and forth, rubbing her breasts against his back with every movement the bus made. The tingling sensation in her nipples increased with every little motion of her breasts against the guy's back. Soon the electricity seemed to be coursing between her stimulated nipples and her aching, dripping pussy.

Monique tried to shift, pulling her upper body back and her lower body forward.

Now, she could feel the ass of the guy in front of her pressing back against *her* crotch. The guy was a young, in-shape art student type, and had a really nice set of buns. Monique felt her excitement rising as the guy pushed back against her.

She pulled away, almost driven crazy with all the possibilities.

But now she was back to square one, her ass pressing against the guy behind her—and he *still* had a hard-on.

Unable to stop herself, Monique leaned forward a little, letting her ass rub against the guy's cock and her breasts press against the other guy's back. *He's going to reach around from behind me and pinch my nipples,* Monique was thinking. *Then that guy down there is going to reach up and guide the guy's cock up inside me. God, they're all going to fuck me. All of them.*

Suddenly the bus driver slammed on the breaks, and Monique lurched forward. She lost her grip on the leather strap and found herself leaning heavily against the guy in front of her. God, that felt good. The guy really did have a nice ass. Then Monique glanced out the window and saw she was two stops past the library.

"Shit," she muttered. "Getting off!" She pushed forward through the thick of the crowd and repeated the phrase three times before bursting in to embarrassed giggles at the lascivious looks of a couple of the guys. "Getting off," she called out one last time, blushing, and stumbled down the steps and through the back door.

She already two stops past the library, so Monique had to walk back she was now going to be even later than she had expected. She had to walk through a densely-packed section of downtown to get to the library, and at every step she was aware of men looking at her, undressing her with their eyes. So the walk didn't give her much opportunity to cool down—in fact, none at all.

Monique entered the office that she shared with Miss Pynchon. Monique was relegated to a tiny desk in the corner, so very much unlike Miss Pynchon's expansive oak desk. Since the two of them spent many hours in here, they had learned to co-exist, and Monique hoped that her embarrassment would pass quickly. But when Monique glanced over and mumbled "Hi," Monique's boss gave her a very stern look. Monique realized, as the older woman's gaze roved up and down Monique's body disapprovingly, that it was as much because of her slutty outfit with the fact that she was almost an hour late.

Of course, neither of these things made Miss Pynchon very happy, Monique was quite sure.

Monique had meant to change her clothes before coming back to the office—but then again, she'd made the assumption that she would have them off for the while she spent at Pietre's house. Indeed Monique had taken her clothes off, but not at all in the manner she'd expected. Monique, perhaps assuming too much, had looked forward to a long afternoon in bed with Pietre, her first lover. But instead, Monique had gotten nothing but a quick wank on the couch, and she hadn't even been able to get herself off before being interrupted by that butler. Then Monique had put her clothes back on in such a rush, she hadn't even *thought* about the fact that she'd be returning to the library looking like a perfect hussy.

Monique looked down as Miss Pynchon said "Your doctor's appointment ran over?"

"Uh...there was a breakdown on the bus," she said, which was almost exactly the truth. If Monique had really lost her composure and lifted her skirt for that guy, that would have qualified as a breakdown. And she had felt that she was going to do it there for a minute.

"Take care that you plan alternate routes in the future," said Miss Pynchon tightly. Monique tried to look away.

"Of course, if you want to plan your romantic liaisons on your *own* time, that would be preferable."

Monique felt a bolt of shock go through her body. She felt sick to her stomach.

"Make no mistake, Monique," Miss Pynchon said, and Monique could feel the old woman's gaze hot upon her, even as Monique looked away. "I have no interest in your private life. If you wish to make yourself a hussy and give your body to whatever man will have you, it is of no consequence to me. If you decide to waste your life lying naked and spread beneath some grunting boyfriend of yours, feel absolutely free to do so. But I expect you to do that *after* hours—not when you claim to be at a 'doctor's appointment.'"

Monique was trying very hard to look away, tears welling in her eyes. But then Miss Pynchon stood up from her desk and walked over to Monique's. Miss Pynchon leaned over Monique's desk and took Monique's face in her hand, roughly turning Monique's head so that Monique was forced to look Miss Pynchon in the eyes.

Miss Pynchon's full red lips curved in distaste as she regarded Monique. Monique whimpered in fear, tears running down her cheeks.

"In fact, I encourage you to be as much of a slut as you can, since that's obviously what's in your blood. I knew when I hired you that you weren't really that mousy girl with baggy sweaters and long skirts. No, the barely covered little tart is more what you are, or I wouldn't have hired you. I knew you were a slut."

Monique choked back a sob. "But—"

"But what?" growled Miss Pynchon, her lips curling back further into a snarl. "There's no arguing about it. If you need proof you should look at yourself in the mirror. You're not wearing anything at all under that skirt, are you?

Monique sniffled, then obediently whispered "no."

"And under the sweater? Nothing at all. Not a bra or a camisole. Just a sweater four sizes too small covering those big tits of yours."

"Only three sizes," whimpered Monique.

"Oh, only three sizes. So you planned this out, did you? You planned the 'modest' look for today. What are you planning to wear tomorrow, just stockings and spiked heels? I'm sure the library patrons would love that."

Monique couldn't turn away; Miss Pynchon was holding her chin quite firmly. But then, to Monique's surprise, Miss Pynchon reached out with her other hand and snatched Monique's long curly hair, pulling at it roughly and forcing Monique's head back. Monique gasped, but didn't dare move as Miss Pynchon looked into her eyes, their faces just a few inches apart. Monique could smell Miss Pynchon's sweet breath, could detect the faint scent of the older woman's perfume. Monique was terrified; she had never been this close to the woman before, and the tangible feeling of Miss Pynchon's authority had never been stronger.

"I—I'm sorry," said Monique. "I won't do it again."

"Oh, that's an empty promise," said Miss Pynchon cruelly. "You'll do it again and again and again. And again and again. That's what a slut is like...she can't help herself, or maybe she doesn't want to. That's what you're like. Did you think I didn't see through your charade at the fundraising party?"

Monique felt ashamed, overwhelmingly. She felt like she would crumble under Miss Pynchon's brutal interrogation. Miss Pynchon whipped off her reading glasses and tossed them across the room. Then Miss Pynchon pulled harder on Monique's hair, forcing Monique's head further back. Monique cried out, whimpering pathetically as tears drizzled down her cheeks. She looked up into Miss Pynchon's face, and for the first time she was struck by how beautiful Miss Pynchon was. The horn-rimmed glasses gone, Miss Pynchon was surprisingly attractive—and Monique, to her utter dismay, began to relax under Miss Pynchon's stern gaze. She felt utterly under the older woman's power.

"Did you think I wouldn't see through that charade? I'm well aware that you weren't wearing anything under that dress—not a stitch. And that you sneaked in here with Pietre Salazar. How did he fuck you, you little slut? Did he fuck you from behind? On your knees or against the desk? Or maybe he did you on all fours on the floor, like the animal you are. Doggy-style, with your ass in the air and your legs spread. Just like the bitch in heat that you are. And did he come inside you? Or did he pull out and make you suck him off? Does a little slut like you swallow?"

Monique struggled to answer. "But...I didn't do any of that with him!"

Miss Pynchon looked savagely pleased by that. "Oh, then he did something else to you! What was it? Did you jerk him off? Did he come into his handkerchief for you? What did he do to you?"

"N-nothing!" Monique was getting incredibly turned on being interrogated like this. The fact that her un-wanted arousal was consuming her made Monique that much more ashamed. This was a side of her employer she'd never dreamed of—and her terror was mixed with humiliation at her own response. She could feel her pussy wet under the skirt and her nipples rock-hard in the tight sweater.

Miss Pynchon snorted in disgust. "What was it he did to you?"

"H-he didn't do anything. Except—"

"Except what, take your ass? That pretty ass of yours? A tight ass like that couldn't open up for a cock like his, that's for sure. You know by now that Mr. Salazar has the biggest dick in the Northern Hemisphere. There's no way it could have fit in your back door, however much of a slut you are. Clearly you're much too tight-assed to accept that sort of thing without a great number of preliminaries—and you weren't in here that long. Unless, of course, you'd opened yourself up before the party—with a few dildos, perhaps? Bigger and bigger until you were slicked up and open enough to take Mr. Salazar's cock in your bum? Or..." Miss Pynchon's face took on a demonic quality as Monique squirmed. "Or perhaps you didn't use dildos at all! Perhaps you knew he would want to use your pretty behind, and so you had a long line of lovers who fucked you there, perhaps a dozen of them, smallest to largest, until you were finally ready for Mr. Salazar's prick—big as it is—did it still hurt when he finally took you?"

Miss Pynchon's face was red with the excitement.

Monique felt her own arousal mounting as she

71

crumbled emotionally under this interrogation. All these sexual accusations were filling her mind with images of the things Pietre might have done to her if she hadn't been a virgin.

"Come on, what is it he did to you? How did you get him off? I know that's all you dream of, is getting men off, getting yourself off. What did Mr. Salazar demand from you? Whatever it was, obviously you supplied it eagerly enough. So what was it?"

Monique felt a powerful arousal rising in her— being called names like this was intensely erotic for her. She could feel her nipples growing ever harder and her pussy juicing with every dirty name that Miss Pynchon called her. But her shame swept through her, and she began to whimper desperately.

"But—but Miss Pynchon, I'm a virgin!"

Miss Pynchon's eyes went wide, and she looked down at Monique with new contempt.

Monique desperately added, "I've—I've never been with a man at all. Not even once!"

Miss Pynchon gave Monique a look up and down, her eyes obviously lingering on Monique's quite evident cleavage.

Then, to Monique's surprise, Miss Pynchon climbed up onto Monique's little desk so she could better pull Monique's head back.

Her knee struck the paper cup of aspirin Monique kept there and scattered perhaps a hundred aspirin across the floor. The pills rolled and scattered over the floor air-conditioning grate, perhaps half of them falling into the vent. Miss Pynchon didn't seem to notice.

Miss Pynchon gripped harder and Monique yelped as she arched her back; then Monique was sliding out of her office chair and the chair was rolling back away from her. As Monique slipped out of the chair, the friction hiked her skirt up, pulling it roughly over the curve of her ass. Monique landed on her knees, her arms flailing desperately; she gripped the side of the desk but, despite her dismay, she didn't dare lay her hands on Miss Pynchon.

Now Miss Pynchon was kneeling on the desk, towering over the whimpering Monique. And Monique was on her knees, head pulled forcibly back, face tilted upward so that she could not look away from Miss Pynchon, who only increased the tightness of her grasp on Monique's curly russet hair.

"I'm sorry, I'm sorry," Monique kept repeating, whispering it over and over again as she looked up into Miss Pynchon's face. "I promise, I won't do it ever again. I'll wear clothes that are more appropriate—"

"No, you won't," growled Miss Pynchon. "You're going to dress like this every day. Look at that skirt, you little slut."

Monique tried to look down, but of course her head was still immobilized by Miss Pynchon's grasp. Monique began feeling for her skirt with her hands, realized that it had been pulled up over her ass, and that even her crotch was exposed.

Frantically, Monique pulled her skirt back down.

"That's better," said Miss Pynchon. "But it would be so much better if you pulled it *all* the way down."

"A-all the way down?"

"As in *off*," growled Miss Pynchon, and a smile broke over her face—an evil, cruel smile.

Monique felt a curious sense of terror flooding through her body. But mixed with it was an intense desire, awakening all the lust she'd felt when she'd been waiting for Pietre to come in and fuck her. She was sure she'd misunderstood.

"T-take my skirt off?" mumbled Monique.

"Start with that," ordered Miss Pynchon. And then pull up your sweater so I can see those juicy little tits of yours. Every man at the party was looking at them. Wanted to touch them. So lift your sweater, you slut, and let me see them now!"

Monique felt a fire coursing through her. She had never been on her knees like this—never on her knees before a woman. She had fantasized for so many years about lowering herself to her knees before men. Now, the dominance of a woman of such power was making Monique more turned on than she'd ever been in the arms of a man—except maybe Pietre. And now Miss Pynchon was ordering her to take her clothes off right here in the office.

"The door's not locked," hissed Monique. "Someone could walk in."

"Then they'll see what a slut you are," laughed Miss Pynchon. "No one will be surprised! Now take your skirt off!"

Monique wanted nothing more than to obey her. The knowledge that anyone could walk in the door at any moment, and that Miss Pynchon didn't care how much anyone saw of her young employee, made Monique so turned on she couldn't have controlled her hands even if she had wanted to. Almost without knowing what she was doing, Monique felt her hands pulling the skirt down.

"That's better," said Miss Pynchon. "All the way. Strip, you little slut. I want to see you stripping down."

Monique took the skirt down to her knees. She lifted one knee, twisted uncomfortably so that she could get her leg out from the skirt; she did this all without Miss Pynchon letting go of her hair. Then Monique squirmed the other leg out of the skirt and knelt there, naked from the waist down, still forced to kneel and look up at her employer.

"Now up with the sweater," growled Miss Pynchon. "Let's see those tits you like to flash to tempt men like Pietre Salazar.

Monique had never before been as sexually excited as she was at that moment. Her pussy was positively dripping, and she knew quite well that Miss Pynchon could probably smell the ripe odor of her juices. Being forced to strip like this was so exciting to Monique that she didn't hesitate at all, but followed Miss Pynchon's orders. She lifted the sweater up over her tits, revealing her perfect firm breasts, just barely too small for a D-cup, with their erect pink nipples.

Miss Pynchon looked down at Monique's breasts, smiling. "They're perfect," she said. "You must like showing them off to all sorts of men."

Monique gasped desperately, "I—I told you, I'm a virgin!"

"I'm supposed to believe that?" Miss Pynchon snickered. "A show-off like you is a virgin? Surely you've had a hundred men between your legs!"

"No, none at all, please believe me," pleaded Monique. "I've never been with a man!"

"Oh, so you've just recently decided that you like cock," Miss Pynchon laughed contemptuously. "A junior pussy-princess, are you? How many of your girl-friends have you gone down on, Monique, then? A dozen? Two dozen?"

Monique sobbed, "No, no, It's not like that—I've never been with a woman, either! I'm—I'm interested in boys!"

Miss Pynchon sneered down at Monique. "You mean to tell me you've never been laid by anyone?"

Monique quickly shook her head.

"How old are you again?" said Miss Pynchon suspiciously.

"Nineteen," muttered Monique, as if ashamed of it.

"Then it's just barely possible," said Miss Pynchon, looking down at Monique's breasts appreciatively. Still towering over Monique, Miss Pynchon reached down with her free hand and began to squeeze them firmly. Monique relaxed in Miss Pynchon's power and savored the feel of the woman's strong hands squeezing her breasts. She was a little gentle at first, but then she started playing with them more roughly, squeezing harder, exactly the kind of breast-play Monique liked to do on herself, the kind that she liked to fantasize about lovers doing to her. Squeezing roughly, working quickly from side to side. Then Miss Pynchon grasped Monique's nipple, pinching hard, making Monique cry out.

"Anyone could come in," she said sternly. "They'd see you on your knees, almost naked, stripping for me. Stripping for them. How would that feel?"

Miss Pynchon's stare told Monique that the older woman was expecting an answer.

"I—I'd just die," Monique whispered desperately, her excitement mounting as she was forced to admit her humiliation. "I would die of embarrassment."

Miss Pynchon worked Monique's nipple cruelly between thumb and forefinger, pinching harder and pulling on it so that Monique's breast stood out painfully. Monique's pain and excitement grew as the pressure on her nipple increased. Both Monique's hands were free, but until now she hadn't dared to place her

77

hands on Miss Pynchon. Now, though, Monique instinctively reached up to grasp Miss Pynchon's hand—but as she did, she found herself placing her hand over Miss Pynchon's—not to pull it away, but to press it closer, in a tender, loving gesture.

Miss Pynchon laughed. "You like it," she said. "The little slut likes having her nipple pinched. You should have them pierced."

"Wh—what?" gasped Monique, barely able to understand through the haze of the powerful sensations she felt as Miss Pynchon tortured her nipple.

"Pierced," said Miss Pynchon. "Bright steel rings pierced right through your nipples. You'd be amazed what that does for sensation. A slut like you would love it. And it would mark you as the sex-slave that so obviously wish to be. Your pussy, too. Do you think you would like that? It's just like having your ears pierced, dear. Except that it signifies your submission. At least, in your case that's what it would do. Do you think you would like that?"

Monique desperately tried to answer "no," but she couldn't. Just the thought of being pierced there, to signify her status as a slave, was arousing her fiercely even though she didn't want it to. She stayed silent.

"So you would like to be pierced down there. Well, I'm sure some day you'll find the proper lover who will pierce your pussy to keep you in line. Now tell me what Pietre Salazar did to you."

Monique looked up into Miss Pynchon's face.

"H-he came up behind me and pulled my dress up… pulled it down…then he started playing with my breasts."

"Like I'm doing?" Monique gasped as Miss Pynchon slapped her breast suddenly, making a sharp jolt of pain go through her body.

"Gentler," panted Monique. "Not as rough as—"

"As you like it?"

Monique felt acute embarrassment, felt the heat in her face. It was true. Miss Pynchon was right. She *did* like it rough. Rougher than Pietre had been doing it. She had wanted him to grope and squeeze and slap her breasts. To pinch the nipples hard and grind them between thumb and forefinger, much as Miss Pynchon was doing now. It was what Monique did when she was alone, and her arousal mounted with the rough treatment Miss Pynchon was giving Monique's tits.

"Not as rough as you want it?" laughed Miss Pynchon, pinching harder so that Monique gasped. "You like it more like—*this?*

Her face flushing still-deeper red as she squirmed with Miss Pynchon's cruel torture, Monique said "Yes."

"Then what did he do?"

"That—that's all," gasped Monique, reacting to the unforgiving torture of her breasts. Miss Pynchon was moving from one breast to the other, pinching and slapping each as Monique gasped and whimpered and squirmed. The whole time, she kept very firm her grasp on Monique's hair, forcing Monique's head back so that her face was exposed and vulnerable. Monique was terrified that Miss Pynchon would tire of her breasts and slap her face—but that fear only kept an edge on her arousal, mounting it higher and higher.

"That can't be all," said Miss Pynchon. "He must have fucked you."

"I told you," groaned Monique.

"I know, I know—maybe it's true. I would love to slip my fingers in there and find out."

Monique shuddered, her eyes wide with desperate need. To her surprise, she realized how much she would like that.

"But I won't give you the satisfaction," Miss Pynchon said. "If you're a virgin, then Pietre Salazar would never let you slip away."

"Wh-what do you mean?"

"He adores virgins. Especially innocent ones who need to be taught to be a slut. You seem to be a natural aptitude...but if you've never gotten fucked before, then you probably need some of his private lessons. You do know that he doesn't donate to the library just because of his good heart, don't you?"

Monique struggled for words.

"Naive little bitch," sighed Miss Pynchon. "Of course you don't. You probably think rich men just get out their checkbooks because they want to help knowledge, blah blah blah. You'll learn."

Miss Pynchon forced Monique's head back still further, bringing a gasp from the helpless young woman. Miss Pynchon looked down into Monique's open, pleading face.

"Open your mouth," she growled.

It did not occur to Monique to disobey. Obediently, she parted her lips. Then, to her horror, she saw Miss Pynchon leaning over her, pursing her lips. From Miss Pynchon's pucker, a shimmering drop of spittle formed, and Miss Pynchon gripped Monique's hair tightly, holding her in place, as it grew. Monique closed her mouth instinctively, and as Miss Pynchon let the drop of spittle fall, it struck Monique squarely on the cheek, splattering over her face.

"Naughty little bitch," said Miss Pynchon. "What did I tell you? Open your mouth. And keep it open this time."

Monique's eyes were filled with tears from the humiliation, but her whole body was on fire with hunger. She was hornier than she'd ever been, about to go completely mad with lust. She looked up into Miss Pynchon's face and obediently parted her lips, feeling the rivulets of Miss Pynchon's spit run down her face and dribble onto her bare breasts.

This time, Miss Pynchon formed an even larger drop of spittle before letting it fall. Monique felt the warm fluid landing on her tongue; she accepted it, feeling a shudder of absolute submission go through her body.

"Good little slut," Miss Pynchon said. "Now get your

clothes back on, and back to work. I expect you to make up the three hours you were gone, tonight. Normally you'd leave at five, so that means you'll be here until eight. See you in the morning."

With that, Miss Pynchon released Monique's hair and got down off the little desk. Monique slumped against the desk, panting desperately and trying to catch her breath. Her whole body was on fire with sex; she would have engaged in sexual contact with any ready man who presented himself at that moment. But she just couldn't beg Miss Pynchon—not after what she'd just endured.

Humiliated, Monique wiped the spittle from her face and pulled her sweater down. Miss Pynchon gathered up her valise and walked to the door. There she paused.

"Eight o'clock," said Miss Pynchon cruelly. "I don't expect you to leave a minute before. And you are *not* to touch yourself in my office, do you understand? I will not have young sluts masturbating in the library. No matter how wet your pussy may be, Monique!"

With that, Miss Pynchon stepped out of the office, locking the door behind her, leaving Monique panting and mostly naked, on her knees on the floor. Alone in that wing of the library.

CHAPTER 5

Monique knelt there for a long time in the quiet of the library office. She knew the library was closing down outside—it was Tuesday, the night the library closed early. Monique could still get out of the office with her library electronic ID card, but she would be alone in the library for the rest of the evening.

Monique desperately wanted to rush home and rub herself madly to an orgasm—but she wasn't sure she would make it home. And besides, Miss Pynchon had ordered her not to leave until eight—and after that display of power, Monique wasn't even going to *think* about disobeying Miss Pynchon. Monique knelt there listening to the sound of her own rapid heartbeat, wanting to reach down and touch herself. But she just couldn't. Not after that order Miss Pynchon had given. Of course, what the old bitch didn't know wouldn't hurt her. But somehow, after the experience she'd just had, Monique was almost physically unable to go against Miss Pynchon's commands. It wasn't that she feared punishment—quite the contrary, the thought of punishment excited her. But she desperately wanted to please Miss Pynchon. Monique had been working in the library so long without giving even a casual thought to what her supervisor was like—and now, in one sudden early-evening experience, Monique had learned more about her than she'd ever wanted to know.

Was this usual behavior for Miss Pynchon? It didn't seem possible, or she would have done this to Monique earlier. Monique had never thought she could have such a powerful sexual reaction to another woman. But in that moment when Miss Pynchon had seized Monique's hair, Monique had absolutely melted in the older woman's grasp. After that point, it was a matter of slipping deeper into submission to her.

Monique was learning, very quickly, that she was destined for a very unusual fate. She had started down the path the moment she had looked in to Pietre's eyes. But she had been destined for it ever since she had succumbed to her first fantasy of bondage and servitude.

Was Miss Pynchon aroused by this power she had

over Monique? Was Miss Pynchon, even now, rushing home to masturbate furiously? Or did she have a partner —she was very emphatically "Miss" Pynchon, so plainly she did not have a husband. But did she therefore have a boyfriend? Or, more likely (in Monique's mind at least), a girlfriend?

And if she had one, did that girlfriend spend evenings on her knees before Miss Pynchon, receiving the same interrogation that Monique had undergone?

Was Miss Pynchon's lover then ordered to satisfy the lusts that had doubtless arisen in the dominant woman's nether regions? With her fingers, or perhaps her tongue?

The thought sent a shudder through Monique's body.

God, she desperately wanted to get off. She was positively dripping on the carpet.

But even though she'd pulled her sweater down, Monique didn't want to put on her skirt yet. She was much too turned on to garb herself in such bulky accouterments. Funny how just a few short hours ago, these clothes had seemed so slutty and revealing. Now Monique longed to be naked, revealed to everyone who wanted to see her. Just the thought that she was naked at work was making her wetter and wetter with each passing moment.

Monique savored the possibility that she might reach down and touch herself. But Miss Pynchon had

explicitly stated that Monique was not to touch herself.
But why should Monique follow Miss Pynchon's
orders—the two didn't have a relationship, and Monique
was not bound in any way to do what the woman said
outside of the workplace.

But this *was* the workplace, and Monique felt curiously under Miss Pynchon's power.

She couldn't disobey, then. She just *couldn't* touch
herself.

Her breasts, though, could she touch her breasts?

Monique played with that thought for a long time,
thinking about the firm buds of her nipples and how
they ached with arousal. She finally decided that Miss
Pynchon must have meant "touch yourself" in the, uh,
euphemistic sense. No, she couldn't possibly have
meant that Monique couldn't touch her breasts.

Monique snuggled back into her office chair, keeping
her legs spread very wide, enjoying the coolness from
the air conditioner on her overheated pussy. Slowly,
Monique lifted the sweater over her breasts again, then
took her breasts in her hands, gently squeezing and
kneading them. Then she started squeezing more
firmly, the way she preferred. She loved the sensation of
squeezing her tits hard, pinching the nipples mercilessly, making herself cry out with mingled pain and
pleasure. Soon Monique was rocking back and forth on
the office chair, feeling her clitoris press against the
rough material. She worked her nipples back and forth

more roughly, moaning softly as she bounced up and down on the chair. God, that felt good. She wasn't really touching herself, was she? God, it felt even better than using her hand.

Soon Monique was moaning softly, slowly mounting the road toward orgasm; her juices drizzled down, soaking the office chair. That's when Monique heard the sudden sound of the key in the lock. Her eyes went wide, and she quickly pushed her chair forward, desperately pulling down her sweater. She leaned her lower body under the desk, grasping for some papers to look busy as the door opened.

It was the cleaning guy—what was his name, Enzo? Something like that. Monique was mortified. She had always thought he was kind of cute. And now to be caught like this—what if he figured out what she was doing?

Enzo looked at Monique, his eyes appreciating the part of her he could see—her breasts, imprisoned in that incredibly tight sweater. Now that Monique had been sweating so profusely while rubbing herself, the sweater looked even tighter and was even more see-through than before. And Enzo plainly liked what he saw.

"Hello there," said Enzo, eyeing Monique somewhat sleazily. She heard his accent and remembered that Enzo didn't speak very much English. Damn. She couldn't even think of a good excuse to get rid of him.

She could just order him away—but that would be so rude. If he spoke better English, or she spoke whatever it was he spoke, she could have made up some barely plausible excuse for needing him to leave the office—personal phone call, maybe. But at this point, she just couldn't figure out how to get rid of him without making it plainly obvious what the problem was.

She felt around with her feet under the desk, seeking her skirt. It was nowhere to be found. Oh shit.

Monique reddened further. She really did want to get rid of Enzo, but he *was* kind of cute—dark and suave-looking, with strong features and a thick mustache. She almost could see herself—

No, that was ridiculous. She couldn't.

Enzo started vacuuming while Monique pretended to work. Enzo kept looking up to catch what he thought were surreptitious glances of Monique's tits, and Monique kept looking over to catch her own looks at Enzo. He *was* really cute, she decided. And those torn-up jeans he was wearing were really tight on him. He had a nice ass. Monique wondered what those buns would feel like with her hands squeezing them as he pumped away inside her—

No, she couldn't think like that! That was just ridiculous! Besides, she was gushing on the office chair, and soon it'd start leaking onto the carpet.

Enzo was working his way around the back of her desk; pretty soon, he would be able to see that Monique wasn't wearing a skirt. Desperately, Monique felt around again for her skirt—but it had vanished.

Enzo paused, noticing the spilled cup of aspirin all over the floor around her desk. Monique tried to snuggle her body deeper into the darkness under her desk, to place the back of the chair between her lower body and Enzo's exploring eyes. She was blushing very deep, afraid that he would see her. As if seeing that she was naked from the waist down would expose her as the slut she was to one more person. Enzo moved the vacuum cleaner over and bent down, pulling off the long tube on the end so that he could more effectively suck up the tiny white tablets.

As he bent down, Monique heard the rattling sound of the aspirin being sucked into the machine. She thought how delicious that suction was, how powerful and erotic it seemed. She wondered what that would feel like if you put it against your skin? Monique shivered slightly as she thought about that. She noticed how like a beast the vacuum looked, like some sort of complicated 1950s vision of a space age robot-monster. Then Monique noticed something else—how cute Enzo's ass looked when he bent down like that.

She realized that she had slipped back a little, her lower body coming out from under her desk. She was fascinated by that ass of Enzo's. His ass was turned toward Monique as he vacuumed up the aspirin, and she could see between his slightly spread legs that he

N. T. MORLEY

had a nice bulge there. Suddenly, Monique's lust consumed her, and she felt a wave of fear that she was
about to do something rash.

At just about that exact time, the vacuum gulped
and whined, sputtered and groaned, and Enzo lifted it
just in time to see the shreds of flimsy black material
disappearing through the tube opening. Monique heard
the fan choking and shuddering, her eyes going wide as
she pushed herself back from the desk and shrieked
"MY SKIRT!"

Then the vacuum, like some mythological beast, gave
a final shudder and went back to running normally,
having devoured Monique's skirt without so much as a
belch. This was an industrial-strength machine, and
Monique's flimsy, slutty skirt had been no match for it at
all.

Enzo looked up and saw what Monique had on from
the waist down—nothing.

In that instant of revelation, of being forcibly stripped
—her skirt now hopeless, useless shreds of material
inside the bowels of the vacuum—Monique felt a
powerful surge of desire go through her.

In one second, the instant she peaked in her feeling
of being exposed—she was filled with longing for
Enzo's body.

She wanted Enzo as she had never wanted any
man—except perhaps Pietre. What's more, she had just
been revealed to Enzo, exposed wholly, ostensibly against

her will. But Monique had known damn well that the cleaning person would be coming in—maybe she had *wanted* to be caught.

Regardless, the sense of being caught now filled her with such an overwhelming lust that she did something she never would have expected herself to do.

She pushed her chair back from the desk, turning it to face Enzo fully. Her legs still spread, Monique was quite exposed to him. Enzo was on his hands and knees before her, much the same way she'd been on her knees before Miss Pynchon. In that instant, Monique sealed her fate with the decision to succumb to her own internal fires. Enzo had long, straight black hair, and Monique reached out, desperately, and grabbed it.

Using Enzo as leverage, she pulled herself closer to him, the wheels of the office chair gliding effortlessly. Monique almost didn't know what she was doing—she only knew that she wanted Enzo desperately, that she would die if she didn't have him. But she didn't want to fuck him—no, as crazed with lust as she was, she couldn't give up that treasure just yet. Against all hope, she was saving that for Pietre.

Monique's rolling office chair came to rest against Enzo's chest with a THUNK as Monique squirmed forward on the chair, and without the slightest hesitation Monique guided Enzo's face between her legs.

Monique was shocked at herself. To engage in such an intimate, enticing ritual—especially for the first time

—with a total, complete stranger, one with whom she couldn't even communicate, gave her an amazing rush of pleasure. And that pleasure was increased a hundred-fold by the fact that as Monique snuggled her exposed sex against Enzo's face, Enzo took the hint and, with an enthusiasm Monique never would have ex-pected, sank his tongue between Monique's swollen sex-lips.

"Oh God," she moaned, leaning back in the chair and spreading her legs wider. She felt his tongue worming its way between her full lips, teasing her virgin opening, licking its way up to her clitoris. Monique's body filled with pleasure as Enzo slipped one of his hands under her ass and gripped the firm cheeks of her behind. Monique could feel one finger slipping into her crack, more from accident from design, and the faint pressure on her untouched asshole made her squirm. The pleasure was unexpected, but it was soon lost in the waves of pleasure coming from Enzo's eager tongue-strokes.

He pulled Monique forward until she was almost off the chair—then he began to give her a pussy-eating like she'd never believed, offering Monique the full benefit of his skilled and talented tongue.

Monique realized she must have hit upon a particular talent—from all the books she'd read, all men couldn't have done her like this. Enzo seemed to have a particular aptitude for this kind of sex, and Monique was simply melting on his tongue, giving herself over to his control, releasing herself into his intense oral lovemaking.

Monique felt his tongue-tip teasing her entrance, flickering her clitoris—Enzo knew *exactly* where to go to pleasure Monique. She ran her hands through his coarse hair, moaning eagerly as he tongued her. Then Monique was pulling him deeper into her grasp, closing her thighs around his face, rocking her hips in time with his tongue-thrusts. Monique felt herself slipping, and then in an almost elegant gesture—without intending it—she slid off the edge of the chair and came to rest on her knees. She pushed the wheeled chair off to one side, and Enzo pushed Monique back onto the carpet until Monique's ass rested against her three-inch heels, and her head was lost in the darkness under her desk.

All of this was unhampered by the fact that the vacuum was still going full-speed, sucking up dust bunnies, adhesive notes, paper clips, staples and the occasional aspirin. Enzo still held the tube in his right hand while his left squeezed Monique's ass-cheeks. Neither Enzo nor Monique gave a moment's thought to turning it off; they were scarcely aware it was still going.

Monique moaned as Enzo's tongue worked her clit and cunt for all they were worth. Monique quickly lifted her sweater up to her neck again, exposing her firm tits. She grasped Enzo's hands to pull them up to her breasts, so she could feel his strong fingers working her nipples, and only then realized that he was still holding the vacuum.

She realized at the last moment exactly what was going to happen. But in that split second, her sexual arousal was such that she would have been unable to stop herself regardless.

The short wand of the vacuum mercilessly seized the firm but pliable flesh of Monique's breast, attaching itself with the suction, sucking the front part of Monique's right tit into the tube. The first shocked scream that Monique gave caused Enzo to start and to lose his lingual rhythm on Monique's swollen clit. In a desperate but chivalrous gesture, he reached out to turn off the vacuum. But Monique grasped his hand firmly, gasping and panting and thrashing back and forth at the sensations the vacuum was causing in her breast. The beast that had devoured her skirt was now, in a sense, devouring her, but the feeling of its suction was causing overwhelming pleasure in Monique's breast. The pain was mingled with the sense of violent pressure, not unlike the way Monique played with her own breasts when she was incredibly turned on. And the feeling of extreme pressure was causing Monique's turn-on to mount, to increase with each second, growing stronger as her distended breast swelled inside the vacuum tube. She held Enzo's wrist firmly and pulled his left hand up to grasp her other breast, guiding his fingers together until he got the idea and pinched it firmly to match the sensation in Monique's other, more esoterically tortured, breast.

The sensation was incredible; she had never felt this kind of pleasure mixed with agony. She hoped she wasn't hurting herself—but God, it felt so fucking incredible. Enzo had returned to his flawless rhythm on her clit, licking down to tease the entrance to her pussy every few strokes, and Monique shuddered closer to her own orgasmic release.

Monique looked down and eagerly watched Enzo opening his pants, hauling out his cock, which looked enormous to Monique. He started jerking off with his right hand, obviously incredibly turned on by the somewhat complicated lovemaking. Monique felt a new surge of arousal—she had always fantasized about watching guys jerk off, but had never been able to do it. The diagrams in the sex books of guys masturbating always turned her on incredibly. And she loved to fantasize about guys jerking themselves off because they were so turned on by *her*. That was exactly what was happening, and Enzo was flogging his prick desperately. Monique threw back her head and moaned, feeling the multiple sensations as she reached her pinnacle. Then she was coming, her hips working back and forth as Enzo ate her. As Monique came, she looked down at Enzo's rapidly pistonning hand, panting "Yeah, yeah, yeah" as she climaxed. "Come, come, come," she panted as she leaned forward, reaching around the tube of the vacuum so she could get her hand close to the head of Enzo's cock.

Then Enzo groaned, his warm breath ruffling Monique's pubic hair, and streams of his come shot out over Monique's hand and onto the floor. She felt the warm fluid spurting into her hand, over her wrist. Enzo finished his own climax and grunted once, pulling back from Monique and then looking up, embarrassed.

Monique grasped the vacuum tube—after the sudden release of orgasm, the sensation suddenly was more pain than pleasure. Enzo reached out and switched it off, and Monique wrestled her distended breast out of the tight tube. She saw the beginnings of a ring of bruises around her tortured nipple—and the nipple looked three times its normal size. Monique was horrified—she hoped she hadn't hurt herself!

To her surprise, Enzo was quickly packing up the vacuum and buttoning his pants. Before Monique could stop him, he had rushed out the door, giving her only an embarrassed glance over his shoulder as he left, closing the door behind her.

Monique shivered. Her body was sheened with sweat, and she was starting to get cold. Why had Enzo rushed off like that? She would have loved to wrap herself in his arms right now.

But Enzo was long gone, and Monique saw that it wasn't even close to eight o'clock. Succumbing to a sudden depression, she looked down, the sight of her naked lower-half reminding her all of a sudden of the unfortunate fate that her skirt had met, devoured by Enzo's industrial-strength vacuum.

This was indeed turning out to be the most bizarre of all Thursdays.

Monique thought, for a moment, that perhaps she should have read her horoscope in the paper that morning—it might have said something.

Chapter 6

Monique got up from her chair and rushed across the office, clicking the latch that locked the office door. She felt somewhat miffed at having been abandoned by Enzo the moment he had gotten off. But she was really more concerned with immediate problems—for instance, the fact that her skirt had been turned to mulch inside the belly of the vacuum cleaner.

Monique began looking about frantically for something to wear. With no skirt and no panties, it would be impossible for her to get home on the bus or even a cab—with a longer sweater, she might have been able to fake it, but there was no chance with this tight one—it barely came to her waist and even left her navel somewhat exposed. Besides the fact that she was wearing nothing underneath it, so it barely even covered her tits. She would have to find something to wear.

Monique went through her drawers, hoping against hope that she'd find a pair of pants or a skirt. Even a pair of gym shorts would be good enough. But to Monique's dismay, she found nothing.

Monique was beginning to panic. What would happen if she couldn't find anything to wear? She felt a curious sense of excitement as she imagined herself walking home half-naked, imagining the looks of shock she would receive. She could imagine herself in such a situation, forced by circumstances to walk naked and exposed through the street, her body available for everyone to look at, to stare at, to comment on, to touch, to feel....

A shudder went through Monique's body.

It finally occurred to her to look in the broom closet behind Miss Pynchon's desk. During the winter, Miss Pynchon hung her coat up in that closet. But this was September, and an incredibly hot September so far. Indian Summer was baking the town, and nobody had worn a coat in *ages*. But was it possible that Miss Pynchon might have forgotten and left a coat in that closet?

To Monique's relief, there was indeed a coat in the closet. But it looked much too small for Miss Pynchon —too short, anyway. Miss Pynchon was quite a bit taller than Monique. This coat was shaped somewhat like a car-coat, but was shorter than would have been right on Miss Pynchon. But then, perhaps this coat was more of a jacket, perhaps only hip-length on Miss Pynchon. Monique couldn't remember having seen her employer wearing this coat—it was a somewhat shimmery purple fabric that belted at the waist. Monique held it up and saw that it was certainly too short for her to wear as an overcoat.

But it would just barely cover her body enough to make her decent. She tried it on.

Just barely was right! Monique looked down at herself and saw that the coat came to perhaps two inches below her crotch, threatening to show off the curves of her naked ass-cheeks with every move she made. She just *couldn't* wear this in public—but then again, what else was she to do? Monique buttoned the coat up and tiptoed down the hall to the rest room. She glanced around the hall for Enzo or one of the other cleaning personnel, but she saw no one. A momentary flare of anger rose in Monique—that was really a nasty thing to do, ditching her like that right after he got off. But God, Enzo's tongue had felt so incredible on Monique's private parts! If she'd known it could feel that good, she would have been even *more* eager to lose her virginity. Monique began to cream just thinking about it, which didn't help her feeling of exposure as she tiptoed into the rest room.

Monique looked herself up and down in the full-length mirror in the bathroom, and she was horrified. The coat was technically decent on her, but it was so short that it showed off the full length of Monique's shapely legs, and it looked more like a stripper's outfit than a legitimate garment for wearing in public. All she had to do was bend forward just a little, and the red thatch of her pubic hair showed between her legs. In fact, she did that for quite a while, telling herself that she was seeing just *how* visible it really was. She leaned up against a stall, spreading her legs slightly and bending forward at different angles, looking back over her shoulder and admiring the way her pussy looked when she exposed it like that. It looked even better if she reached down from the front and parted the lips a little, exposing the ripe pink opening for full view in the glaring lights of the bathroom. Mmmm, that was nice. Monique did that a few more times, playing with different angles as she teased her lips apart. God, it felt so good. After that treatment Enzo had given her with his tongue, Monique was still really wet. And she was getting wetter. Maybe if she bent forward just like this, you could see her juices glistening on her pussy…yes, that's it, she could definitely see it now…framed by the gorgeous curves of that ass….*imagine those guys on the bus if I had been wearing this rather than the skirt….*

Monique was shocked at herself. She found her finger tracing an eager path up her slit, sliding between her well-moistened pussy lips to play with her clit. She whimpered as she felt her aching clitoris hardening as she got more turned on. Soon Monique was bent fully forward, looking over her shoulder to admire her pussy in the mirror as she rubbed it. The coat was pulled up enticingly, revealing all the action as Monique's panting grew in tempo. Monique found herself fantasizing about what she *should* have done with Enzo. She shouldn't have let him get away with just eating her out like that. She should have guided him on top of her and begged for his cock. "Oh, that would have been wonderful," Monique whispered, unbelievably turned on with how dirty and nasty her voice sounded when she talked like that. Especially now, in this public place, knowing full well that anyone on the cleaning staff—Enzo, even— could walk in on her and see her like this, shamelessly rubbing her cunt as she admired herself in the mirror. "I could have gotten fucked right there on my desk...good and hard...I want to get fucked...oh, how I want to get fucked good and hard...."

Soon Monique was moaning at full volume, rubbing her clit faster and faster. She pulled the coat open in front, revealing her tits in the tight, low-cut sweater. Then she pulled up the sweater, hiking it over her tits, exposing her bare breasts so she could give each of her hard nipples a good pinch. She gasped with the plea- sure of that. Then Monique dropped down onto her hands and knees, feeling the cold, slick tile underneath her. She snuggled her ass back up against the mirror, lowering her head so she could look between her legs at the shapely curves of her ass and upper thighs and the way she revealed her pussy when she spread them. She thought her legs looked great spread like that, especially with those slutty heels on. Monique rubbed faster, whimpering, gasping with pleasure, moaning, thrashing. She felt totally unable to control herself—she knew if someone walked in she would fuck them without a moment's hesitation, whoever they were—

Thinking about that, Monique climaxed, groaning loudly, all her shame and modesty washing away in the explosive waves of her orgasm. The sensations shuddered through her body, filling her with pleasure. Soon Monique was spent, her face and her bare breasts pressed against the cold tile, her pussy thrust eagerly toward the mirror, her hand, slick with her gushing juices, hanging limp underneath her.

As Monique's climax dwindled, she came to her senses. *What the hell am I doing? I could get caught in here—caught right in the act of, uh, whatever I'm doing! God, that would be embarrassing.*

But then Monique felt a quiver inside her that told her that the idea of being caught wasn't *only* fraught with embarrassment. It was incredibly hot to her to think about being caught on her knees on the bathroom floor, desperately rubbing herself off. *Would I really have fucked anyone who came in here?* Monique wasn't sure about that one...but at the moment just before she came, she felt that she would throw herself at any warm human body within throwing distance.

Monique composed herself, washing her hands and buttoning up the coat. She took a long, more serious look at herself in the mirror. *This certainly isn't something I would like to wear every day...maybe I'll go back and look through the closet again. Maybe I missed something.*

As Monique returned to the office door, she realized with horror that she hadn't brought her keys with her. That meant she was locked out of the office. She could still get out of the building by paging one of the cleaning staff or a security guard—but there was no way she was going to find something else to wear if she couldn't get back into the office.

Monique sighed, glancing down at herself. *I guess this will have to do.* She would just have to be damned careful about bending and turning.

Monique walked through the serpentine corridors of the library and found the after-hours exit. It was locked, all right. What's more, it was dark outside—it Monique must have been wanking in the bathroom for longer than she'd thought.

Well, now she was going to have to page someone to let her out. Monique felt pretty embarrassed about doing that in the outfit she was wearing—some of them knew her. But there wasn't much else she could do.

Besides, maybe it would give them a different opinion of the mousy chick from the funding office.

Monique picked up the handset and dialed the combination of numbers that sent out a page to the security guard.

She waited there uncomfortably for a few moments, feeling how the breeze from the air-conditioning wafted up her coat, making her feel even more aware of how naked she was underneath it.

Then, to Monique's horror, she saw Enzo coming down the hall. *Oh, brother...why did it have to be him?* Monique was still a little miffed about the fact that he'd ditched her the second he shot his load. When Enzo saw her, his eyes went wide with sudden hunger as he looked her up and down, especially lingering on her exposed legs. Then his face went deep red, his embarrassment evident.

Monique tried to be cool, but as he was unlocking the door, she noticed once again how cute that butt of his was. Enzo paused as Monique walked past him, and for an instant Monique could feel the heat of his body pressing close to hers in the doorway. She saw him lick his lips, and she remembered how incredibly good that tongue had felt sliding up and down in her pussy-slit. Monique quivered. Then she forced herself to slide past Enzo, because she knew if she didn't, she was going to fuck him right there in the entryway, and she was still too miffed to do that.

Monique went out into the street, noticing how a strong breeze had blown up. She kept her hands in her coat pockets as she walked, making sure to hold the coat down so that a stray wind didn't expose her completely. But what was most arresting was the feel of the cold wind on her revealed pussy, especially with it being so wet. Monique's pussy felt even wetter than it had in the bathroom—maybe she had started to juice in the split-second that she was so close to Enzo. Monique chided herself.

If she wasn't careful, this was all going to get way out of hand, if it hadn't already. She was turning into a perfect slut!

Monique walked quickly to the bus stop, well aware of all the whistles and cat-calls she was getting, as well as the somewhat-more-polite looks of interest. Monique felt quite sill about it, but it was really turning her on. She never thought she would get so excited by being looked at like this. Especially when it was something she wasn't supposed to be doing.

All the way home on the bus, Monique had to stand—if she sat down, the coat would hike up and she would be exposed to everyone. She wished she had a bag to lay in her lap or something, but she'd left that in the office. There wasn't much she could do except stand perfectly straight and hope that the bus didn't jostle her too much.

When she finally made it to her parents' house,

Monique almost cursed out loud. Without her keys, she couldn't get in to the house, either—which wouldn't normally be a big deal, except for what she was wearing. Monique had been hoping to sneak in without letting Mom or Dad see her—there was no way she was going to get past them dressed like this without a few questions. What could she do?

Monique finally made it to the house—lights were on, someone was home. She tiptoed around to the back door and tried it gingerly, trying not to make any noise. Damn. It was locked.

There was only one thing Monique could do—sneak in through her bedroom window. Monique's bedroom was on the third floor, but there was a huge old oak outside her window that she could climb up. She knew how to pry the window frame apart just enough so she could slip the window off its track and sneak into the room. She could then put some decent clothes on—a pair of jeans, maybe, or a longer skirt—and climb back down before knocking on the front door.

Only problem was, the coat was much too bulky to make that climb in. What was she going to do?

A devious plan struck Monique. She shouldn't really be doing this, it probably wasn't the most practical thing. But the oak tree she'd be climbing up was hidden from the street and—for the most part—from other houses. So she figured it just might work. Then again, Monique realized she was probably doing this more for the thrill of it than for the practicality. But before she could stop herself, Monique had slipped off her coat and started climbing, wearing only her high-heeled shoes and tight sweater. Those made things more difficult, so by the time she reached the first sturdy branch, Monique had kicked off her shoes and was climbing barefoot. The sweater proved to be too tight and restrictive, though—it kept her from being able to reach very far. So when she paused to catch her breath halfway up the tree, Monique took off the sweater and hung it on a branch.

She knew she must present a rather odd picture, a naked young woman climbing an oak tree in the dark. She felt a twinge of regret that there was no one to see it—it was such a comic idea.

Then, as Monique paused on the big branch outside her window, she realized that she ought to be careful what she wished for.

Her window was *mostly* sheltered from the other houses on the block. But there were a couple windows which faced hers, with a view of the oak tree, and one of those windows had its blinds raised.

Standing in that window, eyes and mouth wide open, was Hank Chamberlain, who had been in her same high school class at the boys' school associated with Monique's girls' school. She hadn't known him well, of course, since the two schools rarely shared

classes and, when the students were allowed to social-
ize together, they were chaperoned strictly. But she did
know that Hank Chamberlain was talked about con-
stantly in the girls' locker room at the community
college. He had supposedly slept with many dozens of
girls. Many said he was irresistible, but a hopeless
rake—never sticking around after the first fuck or two.
Once he got a girl into bed, he discarded her, showing
no more interest. His one steady girlfriend, Megan Carr,
had told Monique when she was a little drunk that
Hank had screwed around on her shamelessly during
the two years they were together.

She also told Monique that Hank had a really enormous dick. "Not that I have anything to compare it to,"
Megan had added quickly and nervously.

Hank had gone off to college last year. A bolt of fear
and embarrassment went through Monique's naked
body. She guessed he was still home for the summer.

Monique flushed hot in the cooling night air as she
tried to pretend she hadn't noticed Hank. She made her
way up to the narrow little balcony outside her window
and began to work on getting the window open. But the
whole time, she was well aware that her naked body
was in full view of Hank Chamberlain. In fact, Monique
could almost feel his gaze on her naked form, hot and
insistent. She had always thought he was so cute, but
the bastard had never given her the time of day in high
school. Well, now, he was paying *plenty* of attention to

her, and Monique felt a curious mix of embarrassment and kinky erotic exhibitionism.

So what if he *was* watching her? He wasn't going to say anything to anyone…not when there was the chance he might get accused of spying…

Monique bent over a little farther than she needed to, so that Hank could get a better view of her ass. She liked that feeling; even if she hadn't meant this to happen, she could certainly make the best of the situation.

When Monique glanced over to Hank's bedroom window, she realized that he'd gotten out his binoculars. Monique could feel her face getting hotter, but it wasn't only from shame. In fact, her body temperature was beginning to rise all over. She slipped her thighs just a little bit further apart, giving Hank a beaver-shot he had probably been hoping for.

Monique almost had the window open, but she lingered on it a little longer than she needed to. Finally, she got the window open and slipped inside, feeling safe and comfortable behind the blinds, but feeling more than a little disappointed not to have Hank looking at her any longer. Knowing that he was watching her gave Monique a powerful sense of arousal, and she was already more than a little wet.

Well, she couldn't just lift the blinds and masturbate for Hank, could she?

Monique shelved that possibility when she realized

that she'd left her bedroom door open. She could hear the sounds of the TV from downstairs. She crawled over as quietly as possible and nudged the door closed. Then Monique inched her way to the closet, where she found a baggy pair of jeans and a sweater. She got into both of those, taking time with neither panties or a bra. Then she found a pair of tennis shoes and laced those up without putting on socks. She got ready to climb back down the oak tree.

At the last minute, Monique remembered that she was going to need a bag or something for all her discarded clothes at the foot of the oak. She dug up an old gym bag from her closet and went out the window again, leaving it unlocked. As she crawled onto the narrow balcony, she was both horrified and pleased to see that Hank still had his binoculars out, and was looking at her quite shamelessly. Once again, Monique pretended not to notice.

She made her way down to the bottom of the oak, then gathered up her discarded sweater, shoes, and coat, stuffing them into the gym bag. Taking a moment to compose herself, Monique rang the bell to be let in.

Mom and Dad were watching Masterpiece Theatre, and didn't have time to ask too many questions. Monique mumbled that she'd had to work late, something about an upcoming fundraising event. Then she quickly raced up the stairs to her third-floor bedroom.

Monique realized as she neared her bedroom that

she wasn't running up the stairs so fast just to get away from her parents before they asked embarrassing questions, like "why aren't you wearing any socks?" She was running because she wanted to get back up to the window and see if Hank was still watching.

As Monique entered her bedroom, she felt a curious quiver of excitement. What if he was? Was there some way she could entice him over here to fuck her? She had always thought he was such a babe...she wouldn't mind him being her very first, even if he had kind of ignored her before.

Truth be told, though, Monique knew that she wasn't feeling especially picky at the moment....her bitterly disappointing experience with Pietre, combined with her deliciously bawdy risk-taking with Enzo, had combined to make Monique desperate for more sexual contact. The fact that Hank was watching her was just another enticing tease.

Monique knelt by the window and peeked through the blinds.

Hank was there, patiently waiting with his binoculars trained on Monique's window.

A shudder of excitement went through Monique's body.

Well, it didn't seem like there was any reason to waste the opportunity....

Quickly, Monique slipped off her jeans, sweater, and sneakers.

She would have loved to show Hank exactly what she'd shown him before—her body, naked and available for him, on display.

But she felt a curious compulsion to do more—now that Hank had seen her naked, Monique felt that she should go one step further.

Or maybe two steps, or three.

Monique quickly turned on her desk lamp, pointing it away from the door so as not to tip her parents off that she was still home.

She quickly went to her door and made sure it was locked. It just wouldn't do to have her parents walking in on her in a situation like this. Then Monique rifled through her meagerly stocked lingerie drawer, finding her prized possessions—still pretty much the only lingerie she owned. She knew she had to work fast—she didn't want Hank to lose interest while he was waiting for her. But she wanted her show to be as exciting as possible.

Monique put on her black lace garter belt, with the black seamed lace-top stockings she'd only worn alone and to the party where she'd met Pietre. The only black bra she had was this one she'd inherited from her older sister Katrina—it hadn't fit her in years. The cup size was *way* too small—small even for a C, which was what the label claimed the bra was (fat chance)—but Monique sometimes liked to put it on when she was alone, since it made her tits spill out all over the place almost like a push-up bra. Monique struggled into it, wrestling her large breasts into their tiny lace prisons. The tight bra forced her breasts together uncomfortably, but the discomfort was a little exciting—plus, it made her cleavage look great. And she figured with those binoculars, Hank was going to be able to see every detail.

Monique put the G-string on over her garter belt—a trick she'd learned from a cheap erotic paperback. The woman in the book had done it so she could take the panties off and get fucked without removing the garter belt. Monique had always thought that was incredibly erotic, and was glad she was finally getting to try it, even if she wasn't going to get fucked.

Finally, Monique put on her high-heeled shoes and quickly fluffed her russet hair. There wasn't much time to fix her makeup or anything; she figured if she waited too long Hank would go back to reading his porno magazines or whatever. Monique would have loved to make herself up for Hank, to put on makeup and tease her hair, to wear the sluttiest lingerie she could find. She was incredibly turned on just thinking about how she was going to show herself off to this guy she barely knew, and she wanted to make herself the sexiest thing she could imagine. But there wasn't time for anything elaborate.

Unable to fix herself to look even vaguely glamorous, Monique opted for the well-used slut look, something she seemed to be doing pretty well lately. In fact, she was getting to like herself this way.

She ran her fingers through her hair, teasing it out so it had that freshly fucked look she so adored. She was finally ready—at least, she was as ready as she would ever be.

Monique peeked through the blinds a little first, just to make sure Hank was still there. Was he ever! He was standing in his window, the binoculars still trained on Monique's window, as if he could see through the blinds. Monique realized all of a sudden that with her desk lamp on, her shadow must have been cast up against the blinds—Hank had probably seen everything she had been doing, in perfect silhouette. So he'd been watching her the whole time, and she hadn't even known it. God, that was hot. Monique was really getting wet now. This was going to be fun.

A thought occurred to her. If Hank was watching her window now, was it possible he'd watched her in the past? Certainly she left her blinds open sometimes when she changed her clothes—in fact, Monique was fairly careless about it. She'd never really noticed that you could see in from that window, and she'd never seen Hank looking at her before. But had he maybe been watching her whenever he came home from college—watching her change her clothes, walk around naked or in her underwear....you could even see the bed from the window. Maybe he'd seen her doing... other things? Monique felt her knees go weak as she thought about the gorgeous Hank watching her stroke herself some time when she'd been careless with the blinds. She imagined him with his binoculars in one hand and his cock in the other, rubbing himself off until he came all over his window. God, how she wished that come was on her.

But more to the point, Monique *always* left her desk light on when she dressed herself up. And she pointed the light toward the window. That way her parents couldn't really see the light under the door, and they would think she'd gone to sleep and not bother her. Did that mean that whenever she had done her... private things—whenever she had explored her nudity in her room, Hank might have been watching her in silhouette, and she didn't even know it?

Monique was starting to ache with need. Knowing that Hank was watching her silhouette, Monique turned her profile to the window and stretched, arching her back so that her breasts were more evident. She tugged down the front of the bra so that her nipples— which were quite hard now from the arousal of these fantasies about Hank—jutted out. Could Hank see their outline? Was he getting turned on?

Monique climbed onto the bed, staying on her knees so that her shadowy profile still fell against the blinds. She spread her legs very wide, and slipped her hand between them in a demonstrative fashion.

She dramatically stroked up and down, putting on a show without really touching herself. But as she thought about Hank watching, she was getting so wet that pretty soon she was going to go crazy if she didn't have at least one little orgasm.

Monique reached out, fumbling for the lever, and casually opened the blinds.

She didn't dare look. She was too embarrassed, she couldn't believe she was doing this. But she could feel Hank's eyes on her, roving over her half-clothed body. She stayed on her knees so that most of her body was revealed to him, rather than being blocked by the window sill. Then she began to touch herself.

Her breasts stuck invitingly out of the bra, so she started touching them. She had her legs wide apart, knowing if she started touching herself down there she wouldn't be able to stop. She wanted to make Hank wait for it. She wanted to make him wait to see her touch her pussy. God, did he know how wet it was? Did he know it was wet for him?

Monique teased her nipples to full hardness, rocking back and forth as she lifted herself higher. She held her breasts in her hands, feeling their weight, their firm, smooth curves. She pinched her nipples hard, gasping a little as the sensation arced through her. She tugged her tits up by the nipples, stretching them and causing little aches of need to shoot from her tits down to her pussy.

Monique was really getting wet. She felt like her G-string must be soaked. She played with her breast some more, then took hold of her right tit with one hand. She knew from experience that she could lift it just high enough to slip the nipple into her mouth and clamp her teeth down on it; she loved to do that when she was making love with herself. But she couldn't get it in with the bra on, so Monique tried for a while, teasing the tip of her nipple with the tip of her tongue, incredibly turned on thinking about Hank watching her do it. Then she made a big slow show of gradually unhitching the bra, which clasped in the front, and easing it off her breasts, exposing her beautiful mounds. She let the bra hang off her shoulders for a minute as she slipped her hand around her left breast and lifted it up to her mouth. This time she could get the nipple in, just far enough for her to close her lips around it and bite it a little, then bite it harder, feeling the tingles go down her spine. She let her left nipple slip out of her mouth and turned to her right breast, teasing that with her fingertips for a while before lifting it in her hand and guiding the nipple to her mouth and suckling it in eagerly. It was harder to get that one in; Monique had noticed years ago that her breasts were ever-so-slightly different sizes. Nothing you would notice unless you looked really close. She had read in one of her pilfered books that most women had breasts of slightly differing sizes.

But Monique so dearly loved to bite her own nipples that she wrestled with her right tit a little, pushing it

119

up harder, finally getting her lips around the hardness of her erect pink bud. Then she was biting down on it, and the feeling of it being a little more difficult excited her, as though she had to work to tease herself. She let her nipple slip out of her mouth, and risked a quick half-glance to her side, feeling a shiver go through her body as she caught, out of the corner of her eye, Hank still standing there with his binoculars.

The window was low enough that Monique could have seen, if she'd had a pair of binoculars or good enough eyesight, if Hank had a hard-on of his own. Did he? God, Monique hoped so. She hoped he was going to stroke himself as he watched her. She thought about his hand going up and down his long, hard cock, and she began to juice even more. Slowly, Monique eased herself onto her back.

Now, with the way the windowsill was situated, Monique's body was partially obscured from Hank's view. So she was careful to lift her legs up straight while she slowly eased off the G-string, taking her time with it, bicycling her legs gently back and forth to better show off their outline with the sexy high-heeled shoes. Monique wasn't too surprised to find that the G-string was absolutely soaked, positively dripping, and after she eased it off over the high heels, Monique lifted it up to her face almost without thinking, and breathed the scent of her own sex. She felt a momentary flush of embarrassment at that, but then that slipped away and

THE LIBRARY

she found herself slipping the G-string into her mouth, gagging herself with the cunt-soaked fabric. She bit down on it as she rolled over and got back onto her knees, her ass resting on her high heels. She let the unhitched bra slide back over her shoulders, and she tossed it back onto her pillow. Keeping her legs theatrically wide apart, Monique let her hand slide down to touch her dripping sex.

The first touch was electric, and her whole body shuddered. She was absolutely gushing, and as she ran her fingers up and down her slit, she heard herself moaning—not softly, as she'd intended, but rather loudly. Loud enough for her parents to hear? *Who cares*, she thought, absolutely taken over by the pleasure of the moment. She teased her clit with her finger, working it up and down, back and forth, flicking it in circles. With her other hand, she pinched first one nipple and then the other, alternating the sensations from one side to the other, shuddering and moaning with pleasure.

Monique finally risked a glance over to Hank, but her eyes went wide and she froze. To Monique's sudden and overwhelming pleasure, Hank had taken his cock out and had his hand wrapped around it. It was hard, and it looked incredibly huge. Monique watched wide-eyed as Hank stroked himself off—then he realized she'd seen him. He dropped the binoculars. Monique couldn't see it all that well at this distance, but she thought she saw him turning bright red. She knew she

121

had to act fast or he would pull his curtains in shame, and she would have lost her illicit partner in this lust-fest.

Quickly, Monique began to rub herself faster, nodding, letting the spit and pussy-juice soaked G-string slip out of her mouth to rest on her chest. She mouthed "Yeah, yeah, yeah" as she worked her hips up and down. Hank stared, astonished, then quickly picked up his binoculars and trained them on Monique. Monique had gotten her message across.

She wondered for a second how good a close-up those binoculars gave Hank. Then, before she knew what she was doing, she had reached out and grabbed the candle from her night stand. Hank was watching her intently, the binoculars moving up and down her body as Monique squirmed and writhed on the bed. She turned her body slightly so that her open, ready pussy wouldn't be directly in Hank's view—much as she wanted him to see every detail of her waiting sex, she was more interested in putting on a convincing show and making him shoot his load for her. God, how she wanted to see him shooting off all over the window. She would do anything to be able to see him cream.

Monique slipped the candle down between her legs, guiding it up to her slit. Bending her body just so—hiding the actual "penetration" from Hank, she began to press the candle along her slit, at a slight downward angle, guiding it down between her ass-cheeks. She did it very slowly, opening her mouth wide like she was moaning and screaming, which she almost did—but managed to stop herself in time. She did herself an inch at a time, shuddering and writhing with each inch she slid between her cheeks. She looked up to see Hank beating off hungrily, slowly and deliberately—not furiously as though he wanted to get off as fast as possible, but slowly, as though he wanted to enjoy every second of his building come and savor each bit of Monique's show.

Monique had never thought this would turn her on so much. There was no way she was going to stick a candle up inside herself—that seemed so unsanitary, and besides, she'd never been fucked—she was sure it would hurt like hell! Monique had read enough true-sex books to know it didn't always hurt, but those Victorian porno books she stole from the bookstore made it sound as though it always did. She wasn't going to take the chance until she was going to do the real thing—why should she? But God, it was turning her on pretending to do it for Hank. She wondered if he really believed she was putting it inside her—from the looks of it, he sure did.

Monique worked the candle back between her cheeks, feeling it touch her asshole. To her surprise, she felt a tingle of pleasure at the pressure of the candle against her behind. Its smoothness felt comfortable in her crack, teasingly arousing between her cheeks. She had read about anal sex, but never thought she wanted to try it. In fact, she'd been sure she didn't want to. She had never played with her butt at all. But for some reason, in this extreme state of turn-on, that felt simply incredible—she suddenly was seized with a wicked thought.

No, she couldn't. That would *really* be unsanitary.

She pretended to push the last few inches of the 12" candle into herself, and started rocking her hips as she made a great show of her ecstasy. And it did feel good— good to act like this for Hank's excitement, even if it was just an act. Monique began working the candle in and out, pretending to fuck herself furiously with it. While she did, she let her thumb rest on her clitoris—just barely pressing, just barely moving with the thrusts of the candle. God, she was going to come soon. She was really going to come. God, God, it was so fucking good—

Monique threw back her head and moaned uncontrollably as she came, desperately trying to stop herself but unable to do so. She thrashed back and forth, pumping her hips up and down so that the candle slid in and out of her ass-crack, teasing her asshole and putting more filthy thoughts into her head. She looked up at Hank and watched as his hand picked up speed on his dick, she moaned "Yeah, yeah, yeah" as he dropped the binoculars again. His eyes snapped shut and his mouth went open, and suddenly he was pumping his dick in a different rhythm, and Monique wished with all her might that she had binoculars so she could see the pearly strings of jizz shooting out of the head of his dick, coating the inside of the window. She looked up at him as he opened his eyes again, and Hank just stared at her with a bizarre mix of embarrassment, remorse, and intimacy.

Monique turned her head to a knock at her door. "Monique! Are you all right?"

She looked back at Hank, who was frantically trying to close the blind on his window—except that it seemed stuck. At the same time, he tried to tuck his cock back into his pants. It seemed that Hank and Monique had each gotten a parental knock on the door at the same time. Monique didn't dare close the blinds now—they made a horrible racket when they clattered down.

"Monique? Are you okay? I heard—"

"I'm fine," mumbled Monique, doing her best to sound sleepy. To her horror, she found that her voice was husky with desire. "I just...uh...I think I had a bad dream."

"All right, honey. Just wanted to make sure you were okay."

Monique looked back to Hank's window; the blinds were down, the lights were out. Playing possum, no doubt. Monique sighed as she carefully replaced the candle next to her door. She pulled down her blind, very careful to keep it as quiet as possible, and lit the candle. She took off the garter belt, stockings, and high-heeled shoes, tossing them carelessly on the floor. Monique lay naked on top of the covers, her hands gently exploring her body as she thought back on the events over this most bizarre of all Thursdays.

What was becoming of her? Monique was desperately afraid of the answer, though the possibilities excited her. She had certainly always fantasized a lot, had fantasized about submission and exhibition, primarily. In fact, it was almost all she did with her waking moments. She had always wanted to be something slightly naughty—well, more than slightly naughty. She had wanted to be something *bad*. A slave. A nude dancer. A porn actress. A prostitute. Anything. Anything that would fill the craving in her body for hard male flesh, on top of her, touching her, enveloping her, possessing her...

But now Monique was beginning to realize that without even being one of those things, she was becoming something at once much more nasty and much more exalted. She was transforming herself into a slut.

"I just want to be bad," she whimpered to herself, looking up at her life-sized poster of James Dean and wondering what his cock would have felt like sliding into her.

But what about Pietre? He had rejected her this afternoon. Was it because of what she'd done—stripping her clothes off and touching herself on his couch? She had been so sure that was what he wanted— perhaps she'd been intoxicated by the moment and by her own twisted sexual fantasies. Perhaps she had gone too far. She had been so sure that Pietre had placed her in that locked room precisely to test her, to see what she would do if given the opportunity. She had confessed to him that she was a virgin, and Pietre had wondered, rightly —or so Monique had thought —if a virgin could really be the proper partner for a man so bold and forceful.

But Monique had plainly misjudged him. She had gone too far, she had been too forward. Perhaps Pietre wanted to be the seducer, to give Monique orders and have her follow them without the faintest impression of her own will entering into the bargain.

It sent a quiver of delight through Monique's body just thinking about that.

Would she get another chance?

Still not knowing the answer, Monique yawned slightly, unlocked her nightstand, got out the plug-in vibrator she'd shoplifted from the department store, blew out the candle, plugged the damn thing in and, muffling the sound of buzzing with three or four pillows, got herself off six more times.

CHAPTER 7

"Monique! Time for work!"

The disgustingly cheery voice of her mother roused Monique from her much-needed slumber. She groaned as she rolled over, then jolted at the sudden buzzing between her legs. She realized that she'd left the damn vibrator plugged in, as she tried desperately to get herself off for—what would it have been, the seventh time? Eighth? No, it was six. She'd had six orgasms. After Hank had closed his blinds. And one before, watching him, with Hank watching her. And one with Enzo, in the library, Enzo eagerly licking at her cunt.

Monique couldn't believe how much her head hurt. She had glanced at the clock at 4:00 A.M.—she'd known

129

all along that it was ill-advised to stay up like this, but every time she'd tried to doze off, she would start feeling the touch of the flannel sheets on her body, feeling the tension in her hips as she eased them back and forth, rocking with the rhythm of her own arousal. Then, next thing she knew, she'd have the vibrator plugged in again and she'd be desperately bringing herself off. This was getting ridiculous! Monique loved nothing more than to go to bed early and bring herself off with the vibrator two or three times. But *six?* If she didn't start getting fucked regularly, she was going to cause a fucking power outage.

"Monique! You're going to be late, honey!"

Monique managed to haul herself out of bed, stumbling onto her knees as she leaned against the night stand. Mmmmm, that was nice. She liked being down here.

No, no, no! She had to go to work. Miss Pynchon had shown herself yesterday to have very little sentiment for young romance. Monique would simply *have* to get there on time.

First, though, Monique was going to have to clean up. Mom would doubtless find all this shit—that would sure be embarrassing. Monique crawled around on the floor, picking up her stockings, garter belt, high-heeled shoes— but then she couldn't find the G-string. She hunted around in the sheets for a while, getting really pissed at herself. How could she go around losing clothes like that? That was the only slutty underwear she had. She looked everywhere but just couldn't find it.

Well, she thought wickedly, *there's only one option, then.*

Monique put away her vibrator and lingerie, hoping that Mom wouldn't happen upon the G-string while making Monique's bed. Mom insisted on making the beds every morning, even when they hadn't been slept in. Well, Monique's bed hadn't been slept in—not much, anyway. Monique wondered nastily if she'd left much of a wet spot.

Monique took a long time in the shower, rubbing the soap all over her naked body, savoring the feel of the warm water and the thick lather gliding over her breasts, her thighs, her ass. She remembered how she'd pretended to fuck herself with the candle—putting on that show for Hank without actually fucking herself. What would it have been like if she really *had* put the candle in her ass? She'd certainly read about people doing it. Monique parted her cheeks gently and let the warm water run over her asshole. What would it feel like to be taken back there? Monique had never wanted to be fucked there, not even a little bit, but now it was starting to appeal to her. She wondered if guys found it gross—but then, from all the reading she'd done, it seemed as though they were plenty eager to do it. She wondered about that.

Monique bent forward slightly, letting the warm water run in rivulets down between her cheeks.

Yes, she thought. *I would let him do that to me. I would let Pietre fuck me there. I would...oh...oh....*

Monique found herself reaching down to stroke her pussy, finding it wet more from its internal juices than from the shower. She knew from much experience that if she leaned forward just so, parted her legs just right, then reached back to pull up on her ass, her pussy was directed right into the spray of the water, from behind, and if she let her mind wander in just the right way she could almost imagine she was being entered from behind—

The water ran down over her clit; Monique repositioned herself ever-so-slightly, and gasped as the stream of water landed directly on her clit—the first time she'd managed to do that from behind. *God, how am I doing this?* she thought. *I'm going to have to draw myself a fucking diagram the second I get out of the shower... oh...oh....*

Then she was coming, almost losing her footing, not even caring if she slipped and hit her head—so long as she finished this intense, almost unbearable, come. She worked her ass up and down, splashing the water over her clit and pussy, as the climax dwindled, the sensations becoming too much for her. Finally, Monique shampooed up her long russet hair and rinsed. She had noticed—for the first time, really—that this particular brand of shampoo had an oddly phallic shape to its bottle. Then Monique worked conditioner into her hair, only barely managing to suppress her desire to back herself up onto the shampoo bottle while she waited for the sixty-second conditioner. She counted out loud: "One-one-thousand, two-one-thousand, three-one-thousand, four-one-thousand...oh...my...five-one-thousand...six....*mmmmmmm*...."

She only made it to thirty because she knew if she didn't rinse that fucking conditioner out of her hair she was going to do something with that shampoo bottle she might later regret. Monique was about to step out of the shower when she reached down and stroked her thighs...there was a faint bit of stubble there. She'd shaved just yesterday, but she so adored the clean-shaven feeling. Monique knew she was running late, but she just didn't care; she was lost in celebrating her body through the many personal care products she was lucky enough to have in her life. Soon she had one leg up on the side of the tub, smeared with shaving cream, as she slowly let the razor glide up her flesh, feeling a faint tingle as she savored the feel of its sharp edge. She ran her fingers over her silky-smooth flesh and was struck with another wicked thought, the latest of many.

No, she couldn't.

Well, if she loved the feeling on her legs, why not try it there, too? But she would have to clip it, first. Monique tiptoed out of the shower without turning off the water, got Mom's nail scissors. She teased her richly red pubic hair out—she could definitely imagine herself shaved. She'd certainly read about it, but she wondered what it would really feel like. She started clipping her pubic hair, finding it a little tougher than she'd expected. Monique worked the lather into what remained of her pubic hair, covering her pussy and just above it, and the upper regions of her thighs. She had never waxed her bikini line, being much less inclined to wear bikinis—or any kind of swimsuit—than other girls at school. But as she began to run the razor over her upper thighs, pubic region, and right up to the edge of her pussy-lips, she felt curious sensations flooding through her. The feeling of the razor on her pussy was newly erotic to her, somehow dangerous and soothing at the same time. She took a long time shaving herself, going over it three times to make sure it was close enough. When it was finally silky smooth, Monique switched off the water and wiped down the fogged mirror so she could admire herself. It felt all tingly and weird—but there was something so sexy about being shaved like that. It made her want to—

Pounding on the door. "Monique, honey! You're already late!"

Damn. Monique had one last thought—she would hate to get razorburn down there. She never got it on her legs, but she sure as hell didn't want to take the chance of having razorburn on her pussy. She found some of that aftershave she'd given Dad for Christmas six years ago. Well, she'd better hurry. She splashed some into her hand and then splashed it over her pussy, letting out a yelp of pain as the stinging sensations exploded in her body.

"Fuck, no wonder he never uses it!"

"Monique—your father needs the bathroom!"

"Shit, shit, shit, shit, shit," Monique mumbled to herself as she searched around for her robe. Her pussy still smarted from that foul concoction. What the hell was in that stuff? She pulled her robe on and limped down the hall into her bedroom, wishing she'd been a little less enthusiastic about her newfound diversions.

Monique looked at the clock and saw that it was already eight-thirty—she really was going to be late. But she really didn't just want to throw on the same old jeans and sweatshirt she usually wore. She looked through her closet and found this loose, airy little sundress she'd only worn a couple of times. It reeked of sunshine, so she never wore the thing—it had been a gift from Grandma. Even though the green and blue went so well with her red hair and green eyes, she had never worn it—it had seemed much too daring for her. But it was fairly short, coming to mid-thigh, and pretty loose—and made of light fabric, so if she didn't wear much under it, maybe she wouldn't get all irritated from that nasty aftershave she'd splashed on herself.

Monique slipped on the sundress without anything on under it—no, that just wouldn't do. She was becoming a slut, but this was a little *too* much. The array of blue and green flowers became distended by the shape of Monique's firm nipples, which were more than a little hard from the shaving ritual. And if she stood in front of the window, you could *totally* see through it. Everything, every outline. Okay, she would have to wear *something* underneath the dress.

Monique took off the dress and stood there desperately looking through her lingerie drawer. Problem was, she didn't really have anything she could wear that wasn't somewhat frumpy. She finally settled on a tank top she'd pinched from her father and cut off just beneath her breasts—and then unwittingly shrunk two sizes in the wash. She found a little half-slip to go with it, short enough so that it didn't show under the dress. Monique smiled as she realized that meant that she could go without panties again. That was lucky, since her pussy was still hurting a little from that aftershave. Maybe she would make a habit of this. Only from now on, she'd be *much* more careful about how she ended up.

Unfortunately, the only sexy shoes she had were those black high heels, which didn't go with the sundress at all. Monique wore them anyway, pleased to be throwing caution to the wind.

Monique looked at herself in the mirror—the tank-top was incredibly tight, so even with the white cotton to hide the outline of her large breasts, Monique felt she looked quite good, and more than a little immodest. The slip kept her from looking like a total tramp, even if the high-heeled shoes equaled things out. Pleased with herself, Monique bounded down the stairs and out into the September sunshine.

It was such a beautiful day, Monique decided she was going to walk to work—through the park. That meant she was going to be *really* late—almost an hour. But something made her not care so much. She just couldn't bear the thought of letting this beautiful morning slip by without a walk through the park.

As she walked down the street, Monique was deliciously aware of the interested gazes she received from men and sometimes women. She felt her nipples hardening fully as a particularly cute guy checked her out. Monique knew that even with the tank top her nipples were probably quite evident now, but it didn't bother her too much—after all, she was going out of her way to wear just what she could get away with. And as she walked, the looks from guys became more open and more interested—perhaps her own arousal was visible to them.

A warm breeze came up unexpectedly. Since Monique hadn't worn panties, the breeze caressed her smooth-shaven pussy—but the lingering residue of the aftershave seemed to perk up and evaporate suddenly, making her newly bare pussy ache with the cold.

Monique drew a sharp breath and squirmed a little as she walked; the sensation was exquisite—painful and

erotic at the same time. She could feel her clit hardening under the continuing sensation, and without the
cushion of hair around it, it felt very different peeking
out from between her smooth lips. Monique had to sit
down on the park bench with her legs slightly spread
for a moment to compose herself. She tried crossing her
legs, but it only made things worse—when she crossed
them, she was acutely aware of every bit of sensation
that differed from before she'd shaved. She could feel
the smoothness of her lips against her upper thighs,
could feel the curious lack where she had barely
known the hair was there. She could feel the pressure
against her engorged clit, and she knew if she touched
herself just a little, she would come, bucking and
writhing, panting and moaning, right here in the park,
with anyone who cared to watch getting a free show.

Monique shuddered. With some difficulty she resumed
her walk.

Now, she was so aware of the sensations of the
breeze across her naked pussy that she could hardly
keep her mind off it. She wondered if all women felt
like this when they shaved, or if it was just her. She
supposed it was the newness of the sensation—but
would it ever stop? Part of her hoped it wouldn't, but if
she sat down and crossed her legs again, she was *never*
going to get to work!

† † †

Monique was winded and somewhat sweaty when she finally made it to the Library. The dress was damp with her perspiration, the cut-off tank top and the slip soaked. All of it clung to her body invitingly, and Monique managed to catch her reflection in the glass doors in front—she looked very good. It excited her to know men were watching her—especially after her discovery last night. She was beginning to feel rather weak in the knees. She felt like she was soaked in sweat, deliciously dripping. And she could feel other moisture, too, forming on the still-stinging lips of her pussy. Monique walked sheepishly into the funding office and met the gaze of an obviously pissed-off Miss Pynchon.

"Monique!" Miss Pynchon hissed. "Do you mind explaining to me why you are *one hour* late?"

Monique stood nervously shifting back and forth, crumbling under Miss Pynchon's cruel gaze. "I-I-I overslept," she muttered. "I'm sorry. I don't—it won't happen again."

"And *what* are you wearing? You know we have a strict dress code against floral prints!"

Monique blushed. She'd forgotten—she didn't *own* any floral prints, and she'd never worn this dress before.

"I-I'm sorry," she blurted. "I'll take it off!"

"What?"

"I mean—" Monique fell silent.

Miss Pynchon stood staring at Monique, her anger radiating. Miss Pynchon had her arms crossed in front of her, her eyes open wide with rage, her lips slightly parted, flecks of spittle forming at the corners. She looked Monique up and down disgustedly, as if overwhelmed with repulsion at Monique's newfound persona. Miss Pynchon's nostrils flared threateningly.

Monique's nipples hardened noticeably. Miss Pynchon was beautiful when her nostrils flared like that.

"See that you do," spat Miss Pynchon, and stalked away into the copy room.

Monique was almost on the brink of tears, but she felt a curious heat coming to her body. She felt an aching need to please Miss Pynchon, and the need seemed to be growing with each second. As Monique sat at her desk, trying to interpret the meaning of that last statement, she felt her mind running away with her. What did that mean? Was she supposed to take the dress off right now and work all day...in her underwear?

In just her slip and the cut-off tank top? Monique knew that was ridiculous, but she couldn't get the thought out of her head. Miss Pynchon was plainly angry, and whenever she got angry she ordered Monique around like a drill sergeant. More than once Monique had felt a curious hunger growing inside her as an angered Miss Pynchon had put Monique through her paces.

Monique couldn't stop thinking about it. She couldn't get out of her head that last comment. Monique imagined herself dressed almost in nothing, ordered around by Miss Pynchon...

What was happening to her? She'd never fantasized about women before. She'd certainly never thought about Miss Pynchon—even though Miss Pynchon was certainly an attractive enough woman, she had always seemed so strangely sexless. Monique had never really thought about those odd feelings that grew in her when Miss Pynchon was angry at her, when the older woman barked orders and expected Monique to obey immediately. She had preferred to ignore them and incorporate her feelings of submission into her fantasies of kneeling down before men.

In the porn books she shoplifted, she always concentrated on stories about women dominated by strong, mysterious, cruel men. Those never failed to fascinate and excite her. But sometimes the books included scenes of women dominating other women—and Monique had always skipped those parts. But what if she were given the opportunity to submit to a woman as cruel and beautiful as her employer?

Monique shivered. That was absurd. Miss Pynchon wasn't interested in her. Not as a sexual partner. Not even a submissive one.

Besides, Monique felt sure she would find it horrifying to be sexual with another woman. To sexually service another woman. Horrifying, terrifying, uninteresting, awful. She was sure of it. Absolutely sure. Positive.

She was convinced she wouldn't find the least bit of eroticism in doing it.

The office air conditioning floor-vent kicked on, and Monique whimpered slightly as the ice-cold wind blew up her short skirt, bypassing her flimsy slip and tormenting her unprotected pussy.

The fan kicked up another notch, then another, and Monique's eyes went wide as the aching sensation of cold increased. .

"Oh God," she murmured, feeling her clit pressing between the tops of her smooth lips.

Then another notch. Monique whimpered "No...oh no...no..." She squirmed in her seat—she desperately wanted to get up, but she was horrified to find that she couldn't move. The unexpected sensations in her pussy had completely taken her over. Monique felt herself moistening, which only made the sensation of cold worse—unbearable! It was as if ice were being stroked rhythmically over her pussy, the slow, sensuous throb of the central air conditioning rising and falling in a rhythm that matched, curiously enough, the pulse of Monique's own arousal.

"Please..." she whispered, "No...."

"I just despise these hot days, don't you?" Miss Pynchon cackled wickedly, the obvious cruelty in her voice penetrating through the fog of Monique's all-consuming arousal.

Monique just barely managed to turn her head to see

Miss Pynchon standing by the thermostat, an evil grin on her face, her full breasts heaving as if with exertion. In one instant, she punched the fan up another notch, and Monique gasped. As Monique's discomfort became quite obvious, Miss Pynchon's nostrils flared visibly. Through the haze of sensation filling her vulnerable body, Monique was horrified to find herself thinking, once again, how lovely Miss Pynchon was, especially when those faint nostril-hairs waved in the wind like that—

"Don't you?" snarled Miss Pynchon, her nipples now evident through the conservative blouse she wore. Monique suppressed a moan as her eyes lingered over them.

Miss Pynchon's whole body convulsed with glee as she cranked the fan up—one more notch, then two. The wind grew to tornado speed, flooding Monique's whole body with agonizing sensation. Her pussy felt numb to everything except the cold and the pain, her clitoris perking up and rising hungrily to catch the breeze, sending spikes of cold through Monique's being.

Suddenly, with the increased speed of the fan, aspirin began to rain upwards out of the air-conditioning vent. Monique gasped as the tiny tablets scattered over her like buckshot. For a moment it was raining aspirin, and Monique realized that one had lodged itself, quite surprisingly, between her ass-cheeks. She plucked it out with some difficulty, her hand lingering over her freezing pussy.

She longed to clamp her hand over it, to warm it, to shield her cunt from the cold, but she just couldn't—she couldn't release the sensation, couldn't give it up. Her hand, as if out of Monique's command, moved to rest on her knee.

Now Monique's nipples were doubly hard, and painfully so—from arousal and from the freezing cold. She felt as though she'd been dipped in ice water.

Monique wriggled her ass, desperately trying to force herself to lift her body from the chair. But she seemed glued to the air-conditioning shaft, her pussy spread and willing above it.

Louder then, more insistent: "I said, *I hate these fucking hot days! Don't you? Monique? Don't you? Don't you hate these hot days? Hate them? Hate hate hate hate hate them?*"

"Oh God," moaned Monique. "No, no, no, no, no—"

"I think the thermostat should be just about right, now—I made a few modifications to it myself this morning."

Miss Pynchon was, Monique had noticed on numerous occasions, quite handy.

"No, no, no, no—oh no, oh no—" Monique gasped, her ass bucking and swaying, lifting off the chair in time with the throb of the fan.

"You don't mind the heat?" bellowed Miss Pynchon, "Not even a little bit?"

"No, no, oh no," moaned Monique. "I love it, I love it, I just love it—"

144

Unable to disconnect from the sensation overwhelming her, Monique spread her legs, leaned forward, pulling her slip up just enough to allow her to press her swollen clit against the edge of the office chair. Mingling with the sensation of the ice-cold hurricane, the pressure of her clit against the chair was just enough to—

"Then again, if you don't mind the heat," snarled Miss Pynchon, slamming the dial back to zero. Monique slumped forward across her desk, her face against the freezing metal, her body hovering on the edge, her whole body shaking both from cold and unsatisfied sexual need. She could come any second, she knew, but now Miss Pynchon was watching her like a hawk—she couldn't let her know how the cold had excited her!

"Oooooh...aaaaaah...oooooh...." Monique cooed, unable to control herself.

"Perhaps I'm just warm-blooded," growled Miss Pynchon, coming up behind Monique and looking over her shoulder. Monique tugged her skirt and her slip down just in time. "You didn't read your memo, did you Monique?"

Monique managed to haul herself upright long enough to look down at her desk. There was a memo there, now hopelessly defaced by a pool of Monique's drool, on official library letterhead.

LIBRARY MEMORANDUM
FROM: Miss Pynchon
TO: Monique
RE: This morning's errand
You are to report to the home of Pietre Salazar, a library donor, at 11:00 A.M., to deliver the proposed blueprints for the new Salazar Wing.

Monique gasped.

"Miss Pynchon—are—are you sure? Wouldn't it be more proper to have someone in the developments office run this errand?"

Miss Pynchon casually sat on the edge of Monique's desk. She reached out and began, in a nonchalant manner, to straighten the low-cut front of Monique's dress, where her thrashings and squirmings had tugged the garment down to expose the majority of Monique's prodigious cleavage.

"Monique," said Miss Pynchon sternly. "I know no one better than you to represent development. Now not another word about it."

Miss Pynchon finished righting Monique's dress and stalked away regally.

Monique felt a terror growing in her stomach, an aching need rising in her loins.

"And Monique?" Miss Pynchon called from across the room.

"Yes, Miss Pynchon?" she muttered hoarsely.

"I expect you to make up that hour this evening. As well as any time you spend on your lunch hour after running this errand. This evening, Monique. Understood?"

"Understood," said Monique miserably.

CHAPTER 8

Monique stood outside Pietre's front door, her body quivering in fear and anticipation. She was a wreck. What if he rejected her again? Monique's whole body ached with desire for Pietre. She wasn't sure she could take it again if Pietre refused to have her. Perhaps she should just turn and walk away. She could leave the cardboard tube of blueprints on the doorstep and—

Suddenly, the door opened. Monique's head pounded. She looked into the face of the butler she'd seen on her first visit.

"May I help you?"

"I'm from the library," she sputtered. "I'm here to deliver some blueprints to Mr. Salazar."

"Come in," said the butler sternly, in a manner that was not an invitation but a command.

"I'd rather just—can't I just give the blueprints to you?"

"I'm sure Mr. Salazar wishes to receive them personally. Come in."

Meekly, Monique followed the butler in the door.

"You've no coat," said the butler, looking Monique up and down hungrily. "But perhaps you would like to leave your purse."

Monique handed the butler the purse; he placed it on a small shelf near the door.

Monique was led down a long, partially dark corridor with rich hardwood floors. Once again, she saw the many paintings of nude women, many of them in suggestive or submissive poses. Monique felt her arousal rising, along with her fear. What if she was told again to leave, without ever being touched by Pietre?

Monique felt tears forming in her eyes as she thought about that possibility.

Monique was led into a small sitting room. The butler indicated that she should wait there, and Monique sat down. She fidgeted nervously as the butler walked through a door and left her waiting for what seemed like many minutes.

Finally, the butler returned.

"Mr. Salazar will receive you now."

Monique felt a shudder of relief go through her body upon hearing those words.

She was led into a large office which smelled of pipe smoke and brandy. There was a large leather-backed chair behind the desk. The back of the chair was turned to Monique.

The butler closed the office door and stood by it.

Monique trembled as she stood before the desk, clutching the cardboard tube which held the blueprints.

The butler motioned to Monique, indicating that it was her job to speak. As she did, her voice seemed to crack.

"Mister...Mr. Salazar?"

Slowly, the chair swiveled around.

Monique almost creamed right there, her knees going weak. Pietre was wearing an impeccable business suit, and he was as gorgeous as ever. His eyes met Monique's, and she crumbled. She swayed and stumbled a little, steadying herself against the desk with her hand. But her eyes didn't leave his for a second. She felt herself falling into them, as if she was being subsumed by the boundless power of Pietre Salazar.

"Yes?" he said to Monique, his eyes leaving hers long enough to flicker over her body—once, twice, a third time. Monique felt her nipples hardening, wondered if Pietre could see.

"I brought you some blueprints," she gasped. "From the library."

Pietre did not smile. "Excellent."

Monique nervously placed the cardboard tube on the desk.

There was a long moment of aching silence, while Monique lowered her eyes, relaxing slightly as she was freed from the grip of Pietre's unforgiving gaze. But now she could feel his eyes on her body, undressing her, possessing her, taking her.

"You'll want to be running off back to the library, then," said Pietre dismissively.

"I—I'm actually on my lunch hour," said Monique, too quickly, and then added with even more haste, "I—I don't need to go back to the library at all. Not this afternoon, at least."

"I see. You're off early on Fridays?"

"S-sort of. I can…I've the afternoon free."

"Then perhaps you're hungry. I can have food brought to the dining room."

"Yes, please," gasped Monique. "I would like that very much."

"Alfred," he said, without turning to the butler. "Show our friend here to the dining room."

"M—" Monique began, about to say her name, introduce herself. But a word from Pietre cut her short.

"No need," said Pietre sternly. "No formal introductions necessary."

Monique crumbled under that gaze. What sort of game was Pietre playing with her? Whatever it was, she desperately hoped it ended up with her on her knees, worshipping him—

"I trust you are not a vegetarian?" It was Alfred, having

moved silently up behind her, so close that his breath felt warm on the back of Monique's neck.

"No," she breathed. "Oh no, no, no. Not at all."

Monique was led to the dining room, where a veritable feast was already set. There was roast turkey, three different kinds of salads, wine, tea, bread...Monique hadn't eaten this well in years. But as she sat down uncomfortably, she realized that there was no way she was going to be able to eat—not a single bite. She was much too nervous, much too afraid—terrified. She looked up at Alfred.

"Will he be...joining me?"

"If he is so inclined," said Alfred flatly.

Monique almost wept to hear that. She was being toyed with. Perhaps it should have made her angry. But all it brought to Monique was a sense of absolute surrender, of being completely, totally, in Pietre's power. Alfred stood watching her eat, his eyes roving over her body openly. Monique managed a few bites of turkey and some salad, but mostly she gulped the wine—two glasses, then three. She started to get a little tipsy. Then, as the warmth flooded through her body, she felt that she was drunk.

She knew it wasn't smart to drink like that, but she was so nervous. She just couldn't bear the thought of being rejected again. Perhaps Pietre was in the other room, waiting for her—spying on her?

That thought sent a surge of sexual pleasure through her slowly warming body.

"Are you sure you're not hungry?" blurted Monique finally, realizing that she was slurring her words slightly.

"I'm very hungry," said the butler, as though it was supposed to mean something, which, to Monique's filthy mind, it did.

"Then eat," she said breathlessly.

"It's not yet time," said Alfred, without emotion.

"When will it be time?" asked Monique.

"When it is time," he answered.

Monique was tiring of this game, suddenly seizing upon Pietre's proxy to focus her sexual energy on. The butler was not a bad-looking man, though he looked at least sixty—if Pietre wouldn't have her, perhaps—

Monique was ashamed of herself. She couldn't just go throwing herself at any man who would have her. Still, he was definitely kind of cute, and the way he was looking at her—

Monique delicately pushed away her plate.

"Finished?" asked Alfred.

"Yes," breathed Monique, suppressing the desire to have another glass of wine. Her eyes roved over Alfred, as she wondered what he was like under that tuxedo.

"Is he going to join me?" Monique slurred.

"If he is so inclined," repeated Alfred.

"If he's not," Monique heard herself saying, "perhaps you would."

Alfred smiled slightly, chuckled.

"I will, my dear. I will. As will many."

That enigmatic reply sent a charge of excitement through Monique's body. Was he saying that—no, it was impossible.

"I'd like to stay," said Monique in a breathy whisper. "I would very much like to stay."

"But lunch is over," he said.

"I want to stay anyway," panted Monique. "Please let me stay. I'll do anything."

"Anything?" asked Alfred with amusement in his voice.

Monique seemed to think about it a long, long time before nodding her head and whispering, "Anything."

Slowly, a smile, an enigmatic, cruel smile, spread across Alfred's face.

"Then come with me," he said.

CHAPTER 9

Monique followed Alfred through long, twisting corridors, struggling to keep up as Alfred led her into darkness. She felt her whole body aching with anticipation—what was going to be expected of her? Would Pietre want her to service Alfred and then him? Would she be taken by both of them at the same time? Would she submit to a flogging, a caning, a spanking? Monique quivered as she thought about all the possibilities, and soon she was very wet indeed. When, finally, she was led into a small sitting room, Monique was almost ready to throw herself at Alfred.

Monique glanced around and saw with mixed curiosity and horror that there were several sets of manacles mounted directly to the wall. She quivered as her eyes roved over them—was she destined to be shackled in them?

There was also a large mirror on the far wall, which meant that Monique could see just how small and vulnerable she looked, and how attractive she was in the sundress. She felt a momentary rush of excitement as she looked herself up and down in the mirror. She felt so revealed in the skimpy dress, so exposed.

To Monique's pleasure, Alfred closed and locked the door, turned to her, and said firmly, "Take off your clothes."

Monique hastened to obey. She slipped out of the tiny dress and let it fall to the floor, then quickly took off the tank top and half-slip. Three aspirin fell out of her top. Alfred looked at her quizzically, and Monique blushed a little.

She stood naked before Alfred, her arms at her sides, revealing herself to him as his eyes roved hungrily over her.

Alfred chuckled. "You weren't wearing panties."

Monique blushed. "I know," she said breathlessly, feeling her arousal grow as Alfred looked over her naked body and took stock of her many slutty habits.

"You weren't wearing any when you came here yesterday, either," said Alfred, looking vaguely amused.

Monique blushed deeper. "How did you know?"

She could see herself in the mirror behind Alfred;

see how good she looked nude. Her breasts were firm
and full, pale; her nipples pink and hard. Her shaved
pubic region looked strange to her, somehow freakish
but oddly erotic.

"You will find that I know a great many things about
you," Alfred said cryptically. "Turn around, slowly."

Slowly, Monique turned until her back was to him.
She could almost feel Alfred's hot gaze on her naked
ass. Was he going to take her there? She had never
fantasized about it until last night, but....

"Keep turning," ordered Alfred.

Obediently, Monique completed the turn slowly,
until she was facing Alfred again. The open lust in his
eyes had increased, and Monique saw with a flutter of
excitement and satisfaction that he was erect and
bulging in the tight tuxedo pants.

"Hold still," he ordered.

Monique's breathing quickened as Alfred took a step
closer to her and reached out to touch her breasts. His
fingers felt electric, his flesh charging hers with an
intense hunger. Monique knew she would eagerly give
herself to Alfred when the time came. He had seemed
so much older when she'd first met him—but now, he
seemed vibrant and even young. If Pietre willed it,
Monique would eagerly accept Alfred as her first.

Alfred's hands slid down Monique's body; he stroked
the smoothness where her hair had been, touched her
upper thighs without touching her pussy.

"You've shaved," said Alfred.

"Yes," breathed Monique. "I...I thought you might like it."

Monique closed her eyes and licked her lips as Alfred's hands returned to her breasts. He took her nipples between his thumbs and forefingers.

Alfred pinched her nipples, so that Monique squirmed and moaned.

"Hold still," said Alfred, pinching harder.

"I—I'm trying," whimpered Monique, unable to keep herself from squirming when Alfred pinched her like that.

"Not hard enough," spat Alfred, and Monique wasn't sure if he meant that she wasn't trying hard enough to stay still or if her nipple wasn't hard enough.

"Put your arms above your head," ordered Alfred, and Monique moved to obey.

"Further apart," he said, and Monique did it. He was very close to her now, his warmth touching her skin. He pinched her nipples harder and Monique writhed in his grasp.

"I told you to hold still," said Alfred without emotion.

Before Monique knew what was happening, Alfred had slammed his body against hers and forced her back against the wall—squarely into the grasp of the manacles fastened securely to the hard wood. Monique let out a yelp of surprise and fear as Alfred quickly grasped her wrists and forced them into the manacles, clamping them shut. Monique was so shocked that she pulled, trying to get free, as Alfred dropped to his knees, getting hold of Monique's ankles and pulling them into the matching manacles for her feet. Monique struggled against the cast-iron cuffs, terror suddenly filling her. But along with that terror was a curious, aching kind of pleasure, a sense that she was soon to be completely fulfilled.

Alfred stepped back and surveyed his work. Now Monique was spread-eagled against the wall, wearing nothing but her black four-inch heels, her naked body displayed for Alfred's appraisal. Monique had never felt so vulnerable, so exposed, so possessed. She was terrified, overcome with fear. But she could feel the warmth rising in her pussy, knew she was unbelievably wet. Her need was growing as Alfred looked her over.

"Such large breasts," said Alfred, touching them. "I imagine men look at them a lot."

Monique sheepishly nodded, her terror overwhelming her. She could feel tears forming in her eyes, but even as they shimmered and drizzled down her cheeks, her desire was growing.

Alfred leaned very close to her. "Such a pretty mouth, too. Full lips." Alfred kissed her, and Monique almost melted. She felt his tongue sliding into her mouth, teasing her tongue, opening her up. She relaxed into Alfred's succulent kiss, giving herself to him. He teased her with his lips and tongue; then, viciously, he took her lower lip in his teeth and pulled firmly.

Monique was whimpering, panting, aching with terror at the power of Alfred's teeth on her lower lip. She felt absolutely at his mercy, completely available for him to use as he saw fit. But still her fear consumed her. Desperately, Monique pulled against the manacles, as if to reassure herself that there was nothing, absolutely nothing, she could do to save herself.

"Please," she whimpered, and Alfred let her lower lip slide from between his teeth. Her lips felt slightly swollen after the rough treatment—they felt puckered, ready, hungry for him.

Would he allow her to pleasure him with her mouth? God, she had fantasized about that. Going down on a man had always been one of the first things she wanted to do when given the chance. Now, Alfred's hand was making its way up her throat, gently cupping her trachea, and Monique slipped deeper into fear and submission as she felt the power of Alfred's hand against her most vulnerable place. His hand traveled up to her face, and he touched her face and lips almost tenderly; Monique obediently nibbled and licked his fingertips as he slipped them into her mouth.

"Skilled tongue, too. I imagine you've had lots of men with it."

Monique completely belonged to Alfred at that moment. She quickly shook her head.

"No," she whispered, more tears in her eyes. "I'm a virgin."

Alfred chuckled. "But surely you've had men in that

way. That is to say, you've used your mouth on them. You've used your mouth to pleasure them."

Savoring the feeling of total confession, Monique shook her head again. "Never," she whispered, and a few warm tears splashed off onto her bare breasts.

"You mean to tell me that a slut like you has never sucked cock?" whispered Alfred.

Monique looked down, as if ashamed. But her excitement was undeniable. She felt that she could come already, if she could just press her legs together a little. But she was well-chained, quite immobilized. A smile broke across Alfred's face.

"Do you prefer women, then?"

Monique shook her head slowly, not so sure any longer.

"You've been with them, though, perhaps you've been with women until now. Perhaps?"

Monique shook her head, quickly this time.

Alfred sighed and smiled, perplexed and enticed. "A virgin in every way, then?"

Monique nodded.

"Surely you've fucked yourself, though," chuckled Alfred. "Perhaps with...a candlestick?"

Monique felt herself blushing deeper, her face hot with shame. How had he guessed that? Was it written all over her face?

But then, she hadn't actually *done* it, had she? Just *thought* about it.

"No," whispered Monique. "Not yet."

"Oh, but you will," said Alfred. "I'm quite sure you will. And with many more things." He paused, reaching up to touch Monique's russet hair. "Your pretty behind's never been taken, either? You've never let a man have you...back there?"

Monique shook her head sadly. She prayed Alfred couldn't tell she'd been thinking about that, too, as dirty as it seemed.

"Some women do, you know. Not very many, but a few. Sometimes a woman will allow a man—her lover— to take her in the bum before she gives up her maidenhead. Something about preserving her virginity. I've certainly heard about it. That could be you, couldn't it? Or are you too pristine for that?"

Monique didn't know how to answer; she felt deeply ashamed of the powerful curiosity she'd felt about her ass last night and this morning. She had even found herself wanting to be taken there. Hoping she would be. It seemed so dirty, but hearing Alfred talk about it so casually, as if it were merely another part of her that he was going to utilize, to investigate, to explore, made her powerfully aroused to the idea.

She could imagine herself pressing back against her lover, receiving his cock into her darkest spot... being taken in that most filthy of ways....owned wholly, even her ass...

"No," Monique whispered. "I've...I've never done that."

"Oh, but you will do it," said Alfred. "You will be taken that way, and many other ways. In every possible way." Monique suppressed a wave of fear and dread; was she really to be taken anally? She felt sure of it. The idea frightened and excited her; she could barely hear Alfred's words, so powerful was her arousal.

"However," Alfred continued, "you must obey one rule if you are to learn all the things we have to teach you. You are under no circumstances to tell me or Mr. Salazar the name you go by in the outside world," said Alfred. Under no circumstances at all. Do you understand?"

Monique was sure she understood. This was so bizarre, it frightened her a little. They were never to know her name? None at all? Even that simple possession was being taken away from her—as the first order of business?

"This is because if you are to continue, you must freely give up your name. You must offer it to me. Do you understand?"

Monique was puzzled. But she could feel her submission growing as she started to understood the extremities to which she would be expected to lower herself.

"I...I think I understand," she said.

"As you submit, which you are doing now," said Alfred, "your name will no longer belong to you. In fact, you no longer have a name," said Alfred plainly. "It is being taken away from you. In your everyday life you may use a name, but it is merely on loan from the outside world. It no longer belongs to you. You are nameless. Do you understand?"

Monique felt the fires of her sexual need rising higher as she was told this. She felt control slipping out of her hands, as she gave herself over into Alfred's power.

"Yes," she whispered, unsure but unable to deny her new lover. "I understand."

"From this point on, until the Master sees fit to allow you to have a new name, you will be referred to only by your number. Twenty-eight."

A wave of confusion enveloped her mind.

"Twenty-eight?" she said breathlessly.

"Yes," said Alfred. "You are the twenty-eighth woman I have brought to the Master. The twenty-eighth woman I have relieved of the burden of her name."

Monique bowed her head.

"Twenty-eight," said Alfred softly, leaning forward to kiss Monique's ear. "Do you understand this? That your name is being taken away?"

"Yes," whispered Monique.

"And you still give yourself to us? You understand that you are delivering your body, your mind, your soul, into our grasp? That we will do with you...*whatever....we...wish....*"

Monique felt that she was drugged with sex, filled

with the elixir of her submission. She felt as if she were reaching her pinnacle, finally being taken over by her desire to live on her knees before her lovers. And now...Alfred was to become her first.

And Pietre after him?

But first, she was being ritually reduced to a number, her being taken away from her. She was being made a slave.

It was as if she were being stripped of her humanity, being taken apart to be reassembled later in an image more pleasing to her... captors.

But they weren't really captors, were they? Monique had come here of her own free will. Or perhaps she'd been manipulated into it...by Miss Pynchon. Was it possible that Miss Pynchon was part of this whole plan? Of course she was. She must be. In submitting to Alfred, she was allowing herself to be used like a tool by Miss Pynchon. And was Alfred just a tool of Pietre's?

Monique shivered.

"Do you understand?" Alfred repeated. "You have no name from this point forward."

Monique nodded.

There was something so perverse, so bizarre, about submitting to this man without ever telling him her name. She felt horrified and enticed by this turn of events.

Alfred's hand traveled down from Monique's face, over her breasts, caressing every inch of her firm mounds. He teased the nipples, pinched them, making Monique gasp. He ran his fingertips lightly over Monique's belly, tickling her enough to make her twitch and writhe uncontrollably in her chains. She pulled against the manacles, feeling more restrained, more helpless, more aroused, than she had ever been. Alfred's hand traveled down to her smooth-shaved pubic mound, and Monique shuddered as he slipped his hand between her thighs, touching the lips of her sex. When he slid one finger up her slit, stroking her unviolated opening, a dribble of Monique's juices ran down over Alfred's finger. He teased her entrance, playing with the tension Monique felt as Alfred explored her. Then he moved up to her clitoris, and Monique groaned as Alfred started drawing circles around her erect bud with his cunt-moistened fingertip.

"You've an enormous clit," he said. "Perhaps that's a sign of unusual sexual potency. I imagine it's very sensitive. Is it?"

"Uh...oh yes...oh yes..." moaned Monique as Alfred flicked her clit back and forth. He teased her further, working her bud with his fingers, seemingly able to sense exactly how close Monique was to orgasm and back off at the last possible instant without letting her come. Twice, then three times, then four times, Monique was on the very brink of her climax, and she was sure Alfred was going to allow her to come.

"Please...please..." she panted, utterly at his mercy.

"Not yet," he growled. "It's not that easy here, little slut."

Then Alfred was pressed hard against her, and Monique gasped as she felt the full length of his hard body, surprisingly muscled and strong, pressing against hers. She could feel the thick lump of his cock pressing through his tuxedo pants.

"I'm going to fuck you so good you will scream," he snarled, biting at her neck and face. "I'm going to enter you so deep you'll feel my cock in your throat. You're going to spread your legs and take me until you're impaled on my shaft—like this—"

With that, Alfred brought his knee hard up into Monique's crotch, slamming against her cunt and clit so that, had she not been chained to the wall, she would have fallen helpless against him. At any other time, the pain would have been unbearable from a blow like that, but from the prolonged teasing she had endured, her entire body was a cauldron of sexual energy. With the hard blow to her sex, Monique's naked body exploded into orgasm; she climaxed as Alfred pounded his knee into her sex again and again and again. She came harder than she had ever come, her entire being on fire with ecstasy. The climax seemed to go on for long minutes, as Monique hung limp in the chains, succumbing to the cruel pleasure Alfred brought her.

When she was finally spent, Alfred ran his hand

down her body again; this time, however, he took his time exploring her. Every movement his fingertips made against her naked body made Monique shudder with delight; her flesh, sensitized by the unbelievably intense orgasm, seemed electric, alive with potential energy. She felt as if Alfred held the controls to her sex and was toying with them, making her writhe and moan and jump as he wished. She had never felt so completely owned.

Monique could feel Alfred's body moving against her as he reached down and unzipped his tuxedo pants. Monique hung limp in the chains, her legs spread wide and her sex exposed and vulnerable, open to Alfred's desires. Though she was upright, Monique knew that Alfred could fuck her right here if he wished, could take her virginity while she was chained to the wall, could explore the unplumbed depths of her virgin cunt with the length of his prick. She felt the head of his cock rubbing against her belly as he wrapped his hand around the shaft.

"Fuck me," she breathed. "Oh please...please fuck me...please fuck me...please..."

"That's right, I'm going to fuck you," whispered Alfred tenderly, kissing her, nibbling at her tongue, teasing her slightly swollen lower lip out—and then taking it between his teeth.

Monique gasped as Alfred bit down—not hard enough to break her skin, but hard enough to tell her that he could have done exactly that if he had the slightest inclination. She felt his arm moving rhythmically against her, as he worked his cock up and down. He stretched up so that his cock touched the swells of her breasts; he was quite a bit taller than Monique, but still had to stand on his tiptoes to get his cock between them. Monique panted hungrily as he began to rub the head of his cock over her breasts. He teased her nipples with it, and she felt the slickness of his pre-come coating her erect buds. Then he was pumping faster, and Monique was moaning "Fuck me, fuck me—" until Alfred groaned and came, and Monique felt the warm, exquisite silk of his jism shooting onto her breasts and belly, drizzling down over her shaved pudenda. She rubbed up and down against him, sliding her breasts against his jerking cock, savoring the feel of his firm body against her. Finally, Alfred came to a rest against her, letting his softening cock press against Monique's come-slick belly.

"But not yet," said Alfred cruelly, and Monique felt an ache in her sex such as she had never felt. She so desperately wanted to be taken by Alfred, fucked by him right here while she was chained to the wall. She would go mad if she didn't get fucked soon—

"Please," she whimpered. "Please. I'm yours. Take me."

Alfred stepped back, tucking his cock back into his pants and zipping up. He ran his hand over Monique's breasts and belly, smearing his jism over her flesh. He lifted his hand to her face, and Monique eagerly moved to accept his semen-covered fingers into her mouth; at the last moment, Alfred thought better of it, and pulled his hand away from her.

"Best to let you wait until you've got a cock in your mouth, properly," he said, and Monique almost wept in disappointment. Was she to be denied even that simple pleasure?

"Please," she panted. "Please let me taste you."

"Oh, it is I who shall taste you," Alfred said affectionately. "I'll savor all the sweetness of your mouth and your cunt. I'll taste it with my hard cock and with my fingers and my whips. I'll taste your mouth and your cunt and your ripe tits and—" he reached back and squeezed her cheeks "—your pretty ass. I'm going to taste every bit of you, devour you with my prick and eat you up with my tortures. But not until the Master has had you."

Monique shuddered, moaned. So she *was* to be taken by Pietre...deflowered on his magnificent cock...and then passed on to Alfred, who would take her as well....

"Perhaps," said Alfred wickedly. "Perhaps. If your submission is achieved properly. If not, then perhaps we'll send you away, still a virgin. Send you out into the world to fend for yourself and end up in bed with whomever you happen across."

Monique looked up at him desperately, pleadingly.

"Please…" she moaned. "Take me now…please…now…."

Alfred produced the key to the manacles from his pocket. He reached up and unlocked the cuffs, then dropped the key on the floor and carelessly walked away from Monique.

"Unlock yourself," he said. "It's time for you to return to the Library."

"But please… "

"You have a great many things to learn," said Alfred cryptically, and indicated the key on the floor between Monique's shackled ankles.

Monique blushed, ashamed of her own need. She would give anything to be taken…to be possessed…to give herself to Alfred and Pietre, to be fucked until she screamed over and over again in release and submission. But she was beginning to understand that she was expected to earn that.

Monique stooped down, picked up the key, and began to unlock her manacles.

Alfred picked up her little half-slip and the cut-off tank top.

"Unseemly," he said. "From now on, you aren't to wear only a G-string. No panties. Ever."

Monique's eyes went wide in horror. "But—but—"

"Not ever. Under no circumstances. A G-string is the only garment allowed to cover your sex. Not panties, or a slip, or anything else on your bottom half. The sole alternative is a pair of crotchless panties once a week—

provided they are French-cut and do not hide any of your ass. But Twenty-eight, they must be crotchless. In addition to the G-string, you are allowed one layer of clothing, and it should not be too concealing. Skirts must end at least eight inches above your knee and must not be too loose. And you must show cleavage, always. Your cleavage will always be visible. Under no circumstances will the neckline of your top rise higher than your nipples. I want your body to be visible to whomever wishes to look at it. Do not cross the boundaries of decency—we can't have you getting arrested—but push them to their very limit. You will wear only clothes which display your body quite plainly to everyone around you. Do you understand?"

"I can't," said Monique, looking up at him with tears shimmering in her eyes. "I don't own any clothes like that." This wasn't, strictly speaking, true—but Monique could hardly wear the same G-string every day.

Alfred smiled.

"Then you must buy such clothes," said Alfred, dropping the bills on the floor. Monique looked up at him helplessly as she wrestled with the shackle around her right ankle. The lock was sticking a little.

"Buy them?"

"Be patient," said Alfred. "I will tell you where to go and what to buy. You will follow my instructions and you will come out looking like the whore that you are."

"I just can't go without panties," she said, blushing.

"I can't go without them all the time...sometimes...."

"All right," said Alfred. "When you're on your cycle, you are welcome to wear a pair of French-cut panties one size too small. Those may have a crotch. But even then, nothing that covers your ass. There's no reason to hide *that* just because you're on your period, is there?"

Monique didn't know how to answer that. She stared up at Alfred desperately, hoping he was joking with her, but knowing full well that he was not.

"You may wear a garter belt and stockings with your G-string—in fact, you are instructed to wear them at all times except when wearing pants. But under no circumstances will you ever wear pantyhose. And you will wear your G-string on the outside of your garters, do you understand? So the G-string can be removed without taking off the garters," said Alfred patiently.

Monique nodded—she'd already known about that.

Monique was still struggling with the lock on the second manacle around her ankle.

She looked at the shackle, exasperated.

Alfred walked over, reached down, and took the key out of her hand. Effortlessly, he unlocked the manacle around her ankle.

Monique felt a powerful wave of excitement at being lowered onto her knees before him, naked.

"As I mentioned, you may wear pants occasionally. But only if they are absolutely skin-tight—nothing at all baggy. And no jeans—only exotic materials, such as

175

leather or vinyl. Or rubber. Shorts are allowed as outer-wear, but only if they are skintight. And if you wear a bra," said Alfred as he towered over her, "It must be one which does not conceal your nipples to much. A demi-bra or a push-up bra of some sort is acceptable. If the bra covers your nipples, it must be made of very thin material. And Pietre informs me that you like wearing a C-cup on your rather D-cup breasts—now you must resort to wearing a B-cup."

Monique's eyes went wide.

"But I'll be falling out all the time!"

"Exactly," said Alfred. "And your nipples must be kept quite evident. They are to be visible whenever possible through your top—whether dress or blouse. Do you understand?"

Monique gaped up at Alfred, amazed at how com-pletely she was being controlled.

"I can't do that," she murmured pathetically, her arousal becoming painful as it grew with every com-mand from Alfred. "I just can't do that all the time, can I? Walk around half-naked like that?"

"Oh, yes, you certainly can," said Alfred. "And you will, Twenty-eight. Your shoes must have heels of at least four inches. We can't have you running away from us, can we?" Alfred chuckled cruelly.

Monique looked down, accepting her fate.

"Several other things," Alfred said, stroking the top of Monique's head. She remained on her hands and knees before him, horrified at all the things she was going to be expected to do before she was allowed to be Pietre's lover—his *slave*.

"Anything," said Monique miserably, her eyes stinging with tears.

"You are to keep yourself shaved down there," said Alfred. "It was so delicious of you to anticipate your Master's wishes by shaving your pussy. But you must keep it smooth for him, always. Your pussy will be shaved each day. But you may refrain from shaving it on Sundays."

"But—I can't do it every day," said Monique, miserably imagining the razorburn she would get.

"There is a store at the Garrison Mall," said Alfred. "On the third floor. It's called PleasureLand. There is a salesgirl—her name is Brianna. Tell her that you're a lover of Pietre's and tell her what I've told you to do. She will give you an ointment that will help alleviate any rash."

Monique hesitated. "I—I'm to tell this woman that I'm shaving down there?"

"Yes. Tell Brianna that *explicitly*. Although, of course, she will already know it. But you should tell her nonetheless. And then you must do everything she says. Obey her command as you would mine. Do you understand, Monique?"

Monique nodded.

Alfred continued, "PleasureLand carries an excellent

assortment clothing which will be appropriate for your new role in life. But downstairs is a store called Flirt!, Next to Nothing, which will provide you with outerwear. Ask for Chelsea at Flirt!. Then, continue on to Next to Nothing, and ask for Alison. And another store in the same mall is called Bonne Femme. There, you will speak to Miss Trustmore. Go to each store and make a pig of yourself, Monique. Then you will visit a store called Chained Heat, on Fourth Street. Visit them in that order, PleasureLand, then Next to Nothing, then Bonne Femme, and Chained Heat last. Cassidy and Kendra at Chained Heat should be able to help you find some clothing which will fulfill our requirements. Cassidy will also have a few toys to recommend, and you will purchase each of them.

"You will tell the sales staff at each store that you are a lover of Pietre's. They will take care of you. You will spend what they instruct you to spend on the clothes you need to keep yourself quite visible. Merely by mentioning the name Pietre Salazar, you will be given unlimited credit."

A shiver went down Monique's spine. Unlimited credit! She had never heard such a sensuous phrase!

"I-I am expected to buy clothes that will reveal me?"

"Yes," said Alfred. "You should look like a slut at all times."

"But my parents..." began Monique.

"This is none of your Master's concern. He and I are

the only authorities about whom you should worry any longer. Exercise great care, Twenty-eight, to keep yourself plainly revealed at all times. Any man who wants a look at you should be able to get one. And any woman, too. But in addition to that fact, you know as well as I do that your parents are leaving today for their vacation. For the next ten days, you are alone in the house. Your exhibition should be quite easy to manage until their return, shouldn't it? Shouldn't it, Twenty-eight?"

Monique nodded. She was blushing deeply, and squirming uncomfortably as she imagined how it would feel, wearing skimpy clothes every day—in front of all those lusty men on the street!

"In addition," said Alfred harshly, plainly tiring of Monique's exasperation. "And this is the most important fact to remember, Twenty-eight. You will not allow any man to take you, until after you have been possessed by your Master," he said. "Do you understand? You are to preserve your maidenhead for your owner to take at his leisure. Your virginity belongs to Master Pietre."

Monique felt her virgin pussy aching as she imagined Pietre mounting her, taking her, as she received his cock into her body for the very first time. She felt a wave of heat going through her body. She was becoming wetter and wetter with every word Alfred said. A dozen sexual images fluttered through her mind, and she suddenly felt weak and faint with desire. Pietre was going to take her, to be her first lover. It was as if her body could already feel its own surrender to the succulent, loving violation of Pietre's hard shaft. Monique began to feel more than a little dizzy as she imagined herself under the thrusting body of her Master.

She looked up at Alfred helplessly, possessed and overwhelmed by her own desires.

"But—But I must display myself? I must show my body off to any man who wishes to look—but I cannot allow him to...to...."

"What, Twenty-eight?"

"To fuck me?" breathed Monique.

"Correct. Men may look but may not touch. Of course," smiled Alfred, "When the time comes, if you prove yourself worthy, the Master will give you to whatever man he wishes. If it amuses him to see you fucked repeatedly by a dozen men, then that is exactly what will happen to you."

Monique moaned softly, her pussy surging with arousal.

"But it is not only your pussy that the Master owns," Alfred went on. "As well, no man is allowed to use any other part of your body until after the Master has done so. Do you understand?"

Monique looked down sheepishly.

"Use my body?" she asked softly.

Monique was wondering if that meant that no man could kiss her. For a split-second there, she had been fantasizing about kissing Hank, who had watched her masturbating. Making out with him. Feeling his body against her. Knowing that she could never go all the way with him. Knowing that she couldn't fuck him. That she could make out with him for ever, even get him off with her hand or her mouth, or let him jerk off onto her—knowing the whole time that she couldn't have him, couldn't receive his cock into her, knowing that she was to be preserved for Pietre.

"Perhaps I have not been explicit enough," said Alfred. "No man is to touch you sexually. No man will touch your body at all. You are to remain a virgin in every way, until the Master chooses to have you."

Tears filled Monique's eyes, brimming over and dribbling down her cheeks. She was bitterly disappointed —how could she make herself a slut if she couldn't even kiss a man?

"I…I can't be with a man? At all? No man can touch me?"

"Yes," said Alfred, obviously irritated. "No man may so much as touch your body."

"Does that mean…does that mean that I'm not allowed to kiss?"

Alfred chuckled with a bit of condescension. "How naive of you. You are not to pleasure a man sexually with your mouth. That includes kissing, doesn't it, Monique? Stop looking so upset. You are being given much more freedom than you deserve. After all, you may still pleasure yourself."

Monique felt a shudder of relief, moments before the disappointment came. Was Alfred saying that Pietre and he could, if they wished, order her to refrain from touching even her *own* body?

Horror, terror, filled Monique as she realized the extent to which she would be expected to follow Pietre's and Alfred's orders. She understood now that they would possess, would command even her most private moments, would be free to order her around in every way, to tell her what and what not to do even when she was alone. Despite her dismay, Monique felt a warm arousal sweeping through her. Even though she was giving up control to that great extent, Alfred had just informed her that she *could* pleasure herself. That brought her an overwhelming joy. If she couldn't make love to a man, couldn't even make out with a man, then she could at least satisfy herself. She could spread herself out on her bed and rub herself to orgasm in full view of Hank and his binoculars, while the hot young stud jerked his meat, sending surges of male lust across the distance between their houses, the heat of his desire flowing across and into Monique's spread and waiting pussy. Monique quivered, thinking about what a whore she would make of herself without ever touching Hank or disobeying Alfred's orders. She felt an enormous, demented sort of freedom, knowing that she would still be allowed to pleasure herself.

Then Alfred continued, and Monique's despair quickly returned.

"Yes, you may pleasure yourself. But you must not allow yourself to climax. You will not climax until the Master gives you permission."

Monique's tear-filled eyes were wide, her mouth opened in dismay.

"Y-you mean—"

"Exactly," snapped Alfred. "You may touch yourself all you want, pleasure your body however you please. But under no circumstances are you to allow yourself to orgasm. No matter how much you might want it."

Monique was gasping and shuddering in confusion.

"Keep in mind, your entrance is to remain virgin, untouched, for the Master's cock—when he sees fit to penetrate you. You may not put anything inside yourself."

Monique stammered, "But—but—but—"

"No, not there either," sneered Alfred wickedly, "You saucy, filthy, dirty-minded little slut. The Master will take you anally, as well—when the time comes, if you have earned it."

Monique looked down, embarrassed. That hadn't been what she had meant, but—now the idea was strangely enticing to her, and she felt an increasing fright to know that this type of stimulation, too, was being denied her. And that Pietre would take her there when it pleased him. Was it really possible for her ass to be used by a man like that? The way her pussy would be used?

She managed to mumble, "When will...when will he take me?"

Alfred chuckled. "That depends on your actions," he said. "It depends on how well you follow our orders. It may be as soon as a matter of months before he takes you—"

"Months!" she choked.

"Or perhaps never," snarled Alfred. "There is much training you must receive before you're worthy to spread your legs for the Master's organ."

Monique murmured quietly, "When will I be trained again?"

"You are being trained every minute of every day," snickered Alfred.

"But...when will I see you...see the Master... again?"

"You will be summoned," was all Alfred said. "When you are ready."

Monique was bitterly angry, but she knew that it was no longer her option to question the orders of her owners. She whispered "I understand," and indeed she understood quite well.

"There is much more that you must understand," said Alfred. "It is important that you know that these are not the only conditions which will be imposed upon you. By giving yourself to the Master, by lowering yourself to your knees before him, you are accepting *all* conditions which he may impose upon you. Upon your body, your mind, your soul, to his total and complete domination. He owns you. Do you understand?"

"I—I think so," said Monique nervously, feeling acutely aroused at the words Alfred was saying.

"Do you understand that you are owned by the Master, that you are allowed no will of your own, no thoughts of your own, that you must obey all of the Master's orders, Twenty-eight?"

Monique bowed her head lower.

"I understand," she said breathlessly.

"And do you understand that if you disobey the Master's orders, or mine—for I am the Master's right hand—if you disobey them even in the slightest way, you will be severely disciplined? Or, and this is important, Twenty-eight, if it should amuse the Master or me to discipline you—whether or not you have disobeyed —then you will be disciplined, with no opportunity to explain yourself or gain a reprieve?"

Monique's sex throbbing as she heard the conditions of her servitude. She would have given anything to be allowed to serve Pietre completely, to give every part of her body and mind and soul to Pietre to toy with however it amused him to do so. Monique could feel herself sinking, slipping deeper into the Master's command. She could feel her will dissolving, her independence disappearing. With every word Alfred said, Monique was giving herself over more completely to Pietre's ownership. She felt like her body was slowly being taken over by the spirit of her submissive self, and that her former life was disappearing.

"I understand," she said hoarsely.

"And do you know that you will be trained as the

Master sees fit, and as it amuses him? That you will be forced to undergo the most unthinkable humiliations merely to entertain the Master for a few moments? And that you will receive no thanks or reward for your sufferings?"

Monique's body twitched. She felt like she tottering on the edge of orgasm as the ritual continued. If she could just reach down and touch her pussy a little—she just knew she would come.

But she didn't dare. She had been ordered not to come—not ever.

She was having difficulty speaking—not because she was afraid, or horrified, but because she was so sexually aroused that she could hardly find the words.

"I understand," whispered Monique.

"And that your body will be modified as the Master sees fit—that if he desires to brand you, or adorn you, or pierce your body in any way, that is his decision, and you must submit to it—without complaint or protest?"

"Pierce?" gasped Monique. Her conversation with Miss Pynchon came flooding back to her, and she felt her arousal rising as she imagined her pussy with silver rings in it. It was impossible—Pietre wouldn't really do that to her, would he? "Would the Master really—would he—pierce me? Down there?"

"Do you understand?" growled Alfred. "If the Master wishes to adorn you in any way—to pierce those pretty nipples of yours, or put rings in your pussy-lips, or pierce your clit or your tongue, then that is exactly what will be done to you? At his command? If it should please him to mark you as his property, then he will do that? Do you understand?"

Monique could feel the ache in her pussy growing stronger as she contemplated that horrible humiliation—to be marked like a slave.

Monique nodded. "I understand."

"And do you beg to be allowed to give yourself over to the Master's servitude and to be treated as nothing but his property? To be fucked and punished and displayed and adorned as he sees fit?"

"Please," whimpered Monique, lowering her face to Alfred's shiny dress shoes. She was down on her knees, her legs spread wide, knowing that the slightest pressure on her sex would make her climax. She felt like she had finally found her place in the universe, that her passion had flowered, her desire come into its own.

Monique began moaning with pleasure as she kissed Alfred's shoes, using her tongue to stroke the slick leather. She whimpered and continuing her begging.

"Please, please Master, please Master, oh please take me, use me, own me." She lavished her affection on Alfred's shoes, worshipping them, caressing them with her mouth.

Alfred chuckled.

"You're very close, aren't you?" he said.

Monique whimpered and nodded. "Yes, Master."

"Reach down and tell me how wet you are."

Monique didn't *need* to reach down and touch herself to know how wet she was—she could almost feel herself dripping onto the floor. But she did as she was told—she reached back between her legs and drew her fingertips up her slit, moaning as she found it, as she'd expected, slick and dribbling with her juices.

"I...I'm incredibly wet, Master," panted Monique. She let her fingertips linger there, at the entrance to her virgin cunt, teasing the tightness of the opening. Her thumb brushed her clitoris and her body shuddered. She moaned—she was indeed very close.

"Thou shalt not come," said Alfred, and Monique's body spasmed.

And Monique came, the light touch of her fingers on her clitoris bringing her over the edge, so that the pleasure exploded and raged through her naked body. Even as she came, the guilt flowed through her; she knew she was disobeying her new owners. And so soon after she'd been given the order! She wept as she lowered her face and kissed Alfred's feet again, making love to the smooth leather of his shoes, paying them homage with her mouth as she thundered through her moaning, shivering orgasm. It seemed as though the orgasm wouldn't stop—it merely heightened, throbbed, grew in intensity and power. Monique's humiliation, her feeling of vulnerability, grew with each second of her climax;

the fact that she was disobeying Alfred by climaxing making the sensation of humiliation even stronger. It was without a doubt the most intense orgasm Monique had ever experienced, seeming to encompass her whole body and spirit. When it finally subsided, after what felt like hours of ecstasy, Monique lowered her hand, finding it slick with juice. She looked up at Alfred, her eyes filled with fear and regret.

"You are forgiven that one orgasm," said Alfred sternly. "But not another. You will not come again without permission," said Alfred. "Or you will find yourself very sorry that you did."

"I'm sorry," whispered Monique earnestly, bending to kiss Alfred's shoes.

"You are forgiven. This one orgasm. Never again."

Monique nodded. "I understand. Please punish me."

"All in good time," said Alfred. "But you are forgiven that single orgasm. If there is a next time it will not be forgiven."

"Please," whimpered Monique, unable to purge her remorse. "Please punish me for doing that. For coming like that."

Alfred chuckled. "Perhaps you can take that task upon yourself."

Monique looked up at him questioningly.

"Perhaps you will choose to punish yourself for your unauthorized climax. To punish yourself severely. After all, you are welcome to punish yourself as much as you see fit. As long as you don't climax, or permanently damage the Master's property—you. Punish yourself, if you feel it justified. PleasureLand can provide you with any equipment and instruction you need to do that. And Chained Heat can give you even more equipment. When you visit there, tell them that Pietre has instructed a program of self-punishment. They will know what to do. Punish yourself, Monique."

"Yes," breathed Monique. "Yes. I will punish myself."

"But still, I have forgiven you."

Monique looked down, her body alive with the excitement of knowing she was going to punish herself for her indiscretion. It was enough to make her pussy start juicing anew, to make the heat grow between her legs...

Monique moaned softly, rocking her hips back and forth. She fought her own arousal, trying to suppress it even as it engulfed her. She *couldn't* let herself get turned on again. If she did, she just knew she was going to come to climax again—disobeying Alfred once more—she just couldn't let that happen!

Then, "Do you love me, Monique?" Alfred asked gruffly. It was merely a game of wills for Alfred, to see if Monique would say these words.

"Yes, Master, I love you," Monique breathed, knowing full well that she did. If not for the person that he was, then for the thing that he represented to her, the thing that he offered her.

Alfred seemed pleased with himself. "Good. A written contract will be drawn up for you," said Alfred. "You will sign it in your own blood. But from this moment, the provisions of your ownership will be enforced. *Strictly*," added Alfred roughly. "So if you have any questions, you should ask them right now."

Monique thought about it for long moments, imagining all the sexual acts she would be commanded to perform, the requirements that she preserve her virginity for the Master. For Pietre.

"You said...you said I could not put anything inside myself," blurted Monique. "Why does that have to include my...my..."

"Yes?" said Alfred impatiently.

Monique was having trouble saying it; she'd never even thought it was sexy until last night. But now, she was aching with desire to do it, to receive a man there. But she was too embarrassed. She couldn't get the words out.

"What are you asking," growled Alfred. "Clearly there's some place that you want to fuck yourself, and you wish to ask my permission. Why does the prohibition include *what*, Twenty-eight? What part of you?"

Finally, Monique stammered, "My—my behind?"

Alfred chuckled and patted her on the head. "Your ass?"

Monique blushed deeply.

"The prohibition includes your tight little ass because,

when the time comes, the Master will penetrate you there with his cock—he will use your ass as soundly as he will use your pussy. If you earn the opportunity to be taken in that manner. Monique, I believe I told you this before, and you are clearly not listening. You are not to penetrate yourself. Anywhere. If you do not show a better ability to follow my orders, I will be forced to release you from service to the Master and cast you into the street. Do you understand, Twenty-eight?" Alfred smiled down at her evilly.

"I understand," said Monique.

"And you accept."

Monique looked down, as if miserably contemplating the fate that awaited her.

But even as she did so, her body filled with an acute knowledge that she was owned, the pleasure of belonging completely to Alfred, and to his Master Pietre.

For the first time in her life, Monique belonged to someone—something she had wanted so intensely.

Finally, Monique nodded.

"I accept," she said.

Alfred smiled, turned and walked a few feet across the room. He lowered himself into a big, plush armchair, and put his feet up on a stool.

"Then come over here," he said, smiling evilly.

Monique was allowed to pay her worship to Alfred's shoes for a time, caressing every seam and surface of his exquisite shoes with her tongue. She became acutely aroused as she did so, and never tired of exploring the sensations of his footwear against her tongue, the taste of the leather and the dirt, the scent of his feet. To her, these experiences were the essence of her new submission, the stuff of her new life.

Monique's worship seemed to go on for hours, hours filled with ecstasy and sexual tension as she floated in and out of peaks of sexual arousal, without ever being allowed to come. Several times Monique tried to lick her way up Alfred's legs, to try to give pleasure to his cock, to satisfy him by pleasuring that so invitingly male part of him. She wanted to take him into her mouth, to learn how to worship his manhood with her mouth and tongue, even though he'd told her that no man was to take her there until the Master had done so.

Even so, Monique burned with the desire to take Alfred into her, to receive his hardness between her lips and taste his seed filling her mouth, gushing down her throat.

But each time she tried to move her mouth up his body to his cock, she was sternly told to return to his shoes, and the wave of exquisite pleasure that went through Monique's body at being told, more than once, to lower her face back to his feet, was like something she'd never experienced before. Like a painful, beautiful kiss. Soon she was so excited that using her tongue to clean Alfred's shoes was all she wanted to do, and she wanted to do it endlessly, until she died here, naked and kneeling at Alfred's feet, her mouth offering hymns to his dominance.

When Alfred pushed Monique away, more gently than she might have expected (or even wanted), he rose and stood before her. Monique saw with great pleasure and a flood of desire that his cock was hard, bulging in his pants. How she longed to swallow it...

"Get dressed, Twenty-eight," Alfred said. "It's time for you to return to work."

Crawling naked across the floor, Monique began to gather her clothes to get dressed. When she reached for her slip and cut-off tank top, though, Alfred chuckled and deftly put his foot on top of the flimsy slip.

"Monique, undergarments are forbidden to you from now on. Now, and forever."

Monique looked up at him and blushed.

"Even the slip?" she asked.

"Especially the slip," said Alfred. Now get dressed.

Monique looked down at the flimsy sun-dress. Still on her knees, she held it up, saw the light from the window streaming through it.

Monique looked at Alfred in shock.

"Get dressed, Twenty-eight," said Alfred with great pleasure.

"But...but I can't wear the dress like this," she said, horrified. "With nothing underneath. It's completely see-through! You can see everything!"

"Then you'll doubtless attract a lot of attention on your way back to the library. In fact, you'll probably make quite a few friends."

Blushing a deep, hot crimson, Monique stood and began to put on the dress. She squirmed into the thin garment and buttoned its few buttons. Her body felt moist with sweat under the tiny dress. She could feel her nipples hardening, jutting out through the dress as Alfred looked her over. His eyes seemed hungry, devouring every revealed curve of Monique's body—and, in the tiny, damp sundress, absolutely every curve was revealed. Being exposed like this was exciting her, even as it humiliated and tormented her. She couldn't walk out into the world like this! Alfred couldn't possibly make her do that, could he?

Surely Alfred was just toying with her. Alfred was going to let her put her underwear on before he sent her back to work, wasn't he?

Monique looked at Alfred desperately. Alfred chuckled.

"Good-bye, Twenty-eight," he said dismissively.

"Y-you can't make me go out like this," gasped Monique, looking down at the tiny, translucent dress. While she was, perhaps, just barely decent, the dress didn't leave *anything* to the imagination! Especially not with her nipples hard like that. The thought of all those men watching her in the street, in the park, in the library...

The thought of Miss Pynchon seeing her dressed—
or undressed—like this—

"Please," she whispered, tears forming in her eyes.
She could feel the sweat trickling down into the small
of her back, drizzling over her shapely cheeks, soaking
the dress where it clung to the smooth mounds of her
ass. "Please," she begged. She could feel her nipples
hard, her pussy wet, her ass smooth and sweaty under
the dress. She was ready for sex, hungry to be fucked.
And Alfred was tormenting her by making her show
her body to the whole world, without letting her get
fucked. "Please," she choked, and felt sweat slicking her
cleavage, soaking the front of the dress, so that it
molded to the shape of her breasts and the hard, jutting
nipples, making them even more obvious. "Please," she
groaned, squirming as she felt the dress moistening still
more with her sweat. She couldn't go out in public like
this. Everyone would be able to tell what a slut she was.
"Please," she gasped, her thighs pressed tightly together,
feeling the ache between them as she realized that
Alfred was, after all, going to make her go back to the
office like this, to expose her body to every man who
wanted to look, to give herself like this to every man on
the street.

"Please," she moaned, offering one last desperate plea
for mercy to the right hand of her new Master, who
plainly showed no mercy at all.

"Please don't make me go out like this," she begged,

knowing full well that she *was* going to go out like this, and that every minute of it would be agonizing, terrifying, humiliating torture.

"Please," she gasped, knowing that she was helpless.

"Don't forget your shoes, Twenty-eight," said Alfred, grinning savagely and holding up Monique's high heels.

Monique was walked to the door, where Alfred retrieved her purse.

But to Monique's horror, rather than handing her the purse, Alfred opened the small bag and reached his hand in.

Monique was too surprised to protest. But as Alfred took out her wallet and began to leaf through it, her eyes went wide in horror.

Still, she dared not say a word.

Alfred found her bus pass and took it out of her wallet. Then, casually, he counted the twenty-four dollars Monique had in her wallet. Then he fished out her ATM card. Alfred tucked it all into his pocket along with the bus pass, and handed Monique back her purse.

"Wh-what are you doing?" she said, mortified.

"I think you'd be better walking," said Alfred with a wicked grin. "Exercise is good for you."

Monique felt a surge of fear; he was making her walk so that more men would see her. She would be even more exposed, more revealed. She couldn't even hide out in the back of the bus. She would have to walk the whole way back to the library...and *everyone* would see her!

But Monique, despite her horror at this treatment, felt her arousal more strongly than ever. She looked at Alfred and felt more possessed by him than ever. Every indignity she was made to suffer made Monique ache with desire for the next. For they were all marks of her submission, parts of her new life on her knees before Pietre.

"When will I see you again?" she asked desperately.

"Never," chuckled Alfred. "Or always. You are not to come here without being summoned."

"How...when will I be summoned?"

Alfred sneered at Monique, not even dignifying her last query with an answer. He opened the door and said, "Good-bye, Twenty-eight."

Sadly, Monique walked through the door and back into the world.

CHAPTER 10

Walking back to work through the park was every bit of torture that Monique had thought it was going to be. In the light of the late afternoon, she felt as though the dress was completely see-through, and, in fact, it was. She felt as though every man she passed was undressing her with his eyes, was savoring the lines of her body under the flimsy, tiny dress. She could feel the heat of their stares roving over her body, touching her breasts, her nipples, her sex, her belly, her ass, her thighs. She could feel them taking her dress off and touching her body with their lustful glances, teasing her erect nipples and spreading their legs with their hungry stares, mounting her, pushing inside her, fucking her deeply with their demanding looks—

Monique felt as if she was being taken by all these men at once. She ached with the pleasure of it; her body hummed with desire. Monique felt as if she had been given to all these men to be used as they saw fit. Being forced to exhibit herself like this, Monique knew she was being tormented—Alfred, and probably Pietre, knew how exposed and vulnerable she would feel doing this. But the exquisite, agonizing pleasure that was flowing through Monique's body, the ecstasy of her humiliation, was its own kind of torture for Monique. Soon Monique was panting and wet as she walked along the tree-lined paths. Monique could feel the curves of her body being traced by the hot gazes of the men, and her sex ached and throbbed with every caress. She could feel them touching her, invading her, owning her, possessing her—

Monique had to stop and sit down on a park bench, or she was going to hyperventilate. She sat there, feeling the cool wood of the bench against her buttocks and upper thighs. She was near a small fountain, and she could feel the spray of the water gently caressing her flesh.

A man, rather old and bedraggled, wearing a filthy black overcoat much too hot for the weather, surprised Monique as he appeared right next to her. He must have come from behind, maybe walking through the bushes along one of the lesser-used trails.

Monique looked at the dirty man for a moment,

dumbfounded. He was just a couple of feet away from her, standing with a big wide grin on his face—he was missing several teeth. Monique looked up at his face; his eyes roved up and down over her body. He was drinking in the sight of her erect nipples pushing through the thin material of the dress; he devoured the curve of her legs.

Then, in one smooth, sudden movement, the man opened his raincoat, revealing a filthy shirt and filthy pair of pants, with the fly open and a shockingly large, erect, glistening penis jutting out.

Monique gasped, stunned, and just stared, wide-eyed and gape-mouthed. The old man's dick must have been at least ten inches long, and thick; Monique hadn't had much experience with men's organs, but this one looked huge, even a little scary. Monique was so shocked that she just watched as the man held his coat open with one hand while he wrapped the other hand, filthy and scabbed, around his big cock. He began to jerk himself off furiously as Monique stared.

Monique was suddenly fascinated by the way the man's hand pumped his huge cock—she hadn't imagined that guys could move that fast while they jerked off. *God, I wish my hand could move that fast when I'm doing myself. Look at that. God, he's staring at me.* Monique looked up at him, dumbfounded, as the man waited for her to be shocked, dismayed, horrified.

But it took almost half a minute before Monique realized that she *was* sort of dismayed, horrified— not because the guy was jerking off in her face, but because the whole situation was so *weird.*

She looked at the guy's hand furiously pumping his cock, then up at his face, seeing the demented smile as he laughed with glee. Then Monique looked back down at his cock.

Monique realized that several people had gathered around, gasping and pointing, expressing how offended they were. The guy seemed to be picking up speed, wanking faster as the small crowd started heaping ridicule on him.

Monique's eyes lingered over his pumping hand, his hard cock—then she looked back up at his face, the horror, the repulsion, suddenly dawning on her.

She looked into the guy's bloodshot eyes, saw the pure bliss on them as he laughed maniacally.

Back at his cock. Back into his face.

"Ew," Monique finally said, her face twisted in disgust.

At that moment, as Monique's repulsion brimmed over her face, the guy finally let himself go, grunting and groaning as streams of jizz shot out and slicked the ground immediately before Monique. She almost thought she felt a brief squirt hit her hand, but when she desperately tried to rub it off, she couldn't find it and thought it was just her imagination.

The guy finished jerking off, his hand now slick and

shimmering with come. He quickly tucked his prick away and ran off into the bushes.

People were crowding around Monique, mostly guys. "Hey lady, you okay?" "What did he do to you?" "He just took his dick out and started jerking off like that?" "Disgusting!" "He almost came all over her!" "The animal!" It took a few seconds for Monique to return to reality. Then she suddenly looked around and saw that she was surrounded by men, all crowded close and asking her about the guy whose cock had just been in her face. Monique felt a sudden rush of heat as she recognized the looks in the eyes of the men; they had crowded close to her in concern, but then as they pressed closer and realized she was all right, their looks changed from concern to hunger. They were so close. All around her. Monique could feel their heat. Could feel the sweat soaking her dress. Could feel their eyes on her breasts. Touching the hard nipples. Could feel them taking off her dress. Stripping her. She could feel them lifting her skirt, spreading her legs, mounting her—

"I—I'm fine," she said hoarsely, her pussy aching and so wet that she was afraid she couldn't get up for fear of leaving a wet spot on the bench. "Really," she said, looking at the guys who surrounded her, feeling their desire, their need for her. "Really, I'm fine. I'm fine, really." She was breathing heavily, flushed a deep red, her nipples painful in their hardness and her pussy juicing between her tightly-closed thighs. Monique felt an arm on her shoulder.

"Perhaps I could give you a ride to the police station," said a handsome, dignified-looking man in an expensive business suit. "My car is parked right over here."

Monique could feel them closing in, pressing around her, men in suits walking through the park on their way home from work, or their way to the gym. She could feel them surrounding her, undressing her, taking her one by one, or taking her all at once, one in her mouth, one in her pussy, one in each hand....one in her ass....

Monique felt a rush as she realized that the man who had offered her a ride was rather good-looking, and his concern seemed quite genuine. His eyes weren't roving over her body the way the other men's were, weren't touching her all over, drinking in her beauty....weren't trying to look down her dress, see her breasts and her cleavage...not the way all the other men were....this guy was so cute...he would do to start...and all the others could join him once he'd gotten Monique warmed up... then again, maybe she didn't need to be warmed up....

Monique shook her head, trying to clear it. She had to get out of here. She was losing control.

"Can I give you a ride?" the good-looking man repeated. "To the police station? You should file a report."

"Yes, panted Monique, trying to make her heat- and sex-flush seem like distress, as if she was about to cry from the indignity of it all. "Yes," she whimpered desperately. "I think you'd better give me a ride."

Monique had some difficulty walking, but she managed to make it to the guy's car. The car was a Jaguar, brand new, and parked illegally in a blue zone. Monique needed help from the guy to get into the passenger's seat. The guy got in and reached over to touch her shoulder, his face filled with concern.

"Are you all right?" he asked earnestly. "That was horrible. That any woman should be subjected to that—it's disgusting."

Monique could smell the man's cologne, could feel his warmth.

"Yes," she panted. "It—it was horrible. I thought—"

"You should file a report," said the man. "I'll take you right to the police station." He started the car.

"Buckle your seatbelt," he told Monique with overstated concern.

With fumbling hands, Monique tried to obey. When it became clear there was no way she was going to be able to get the seatbelt fastened, the guy leaned over and helped her get the belt strapped across her lap. The guy leaned against Monique a little, and she could feel one nipple tingling as his shoulder brushed it. Monique could smell his sweat mingled with the cologne, could imagine what it would smell like if he had been sweating on top of a woman for hours— sweating on top of Monique—fucking her, pushing into her, pumping her, penetrating her, filling her with his hard flesh—

"There we go," the man said with some discomfort. The shoulder belt slide neatly between Monique's breasts.

"Right to the police station," said the man, for the first time showing a little difficulty. He cleared his throat and pulled at his collar, as if it was choking him.

"Right to the police station," he repeated nervously as he pulled out into traffic.

"Yes, oh yes," said Monique, her voice breathy and rough. "I want to tell them everything...."

The man's name was Phil, and he was a lawyer. A successful one, from the looks of the car and the suit. He stayed with Monique as she filed her report, describing every detail—except the way that the press of men had made her body react, had made her desire rise.

"It was horrible," she managed to murmur, finally. What she didn't tell the cop was that what was horrible was the fact that she'd been forced to restrain herself when the men had crowded around her.

The cop who interviewed her kept looking her over, up and down, taking in every curve, every slope of her body, enjoying the view. He wasn't too bad looking, either, and Monique found herself savoring the sight of his eyes lingering over her breasts and her thighs and her ass. When she went out into the squad room, it wasn't just the one cop who looked her over, but it was all of them. Soon she was hopelessly wet again.

"I...I could use a ride back to work," she said breathlessly, looking at Phil meaningfully.

Phil led her out to his Jaguar and helped her into the seatbelt again, this time being a little less careful to avoid brushing against her body, maybe spending a little less effort to make sure his hands didn't linger as he straightened the shoulder belt by sliding his hand up it, just inches away from Monique's breasts.

By that time it was early evening, and Monique realized with some fright that there was no point in going back to work. Miss Pynchon was long gone, the library would be empty. Monique blushed as she realized that she would be in big trouble for not having come back to work at all. Miss Pynchon had told her she would be expected to make up her time out of the office—that very evening. Now she wasn't even going to be there at all.

But it was Friday night, now, and Monique didn't have to go back to the library until Monday. She felt a wave of fear as she contemplated the weekend before her.

She had been ordered to let no man touch her. To let no man take her.

And now she had two full days without work, forty-eight hours of unstructured time. Could she control herself?

Monique had spent her life as a virgin until now. But for some reason, at this moment, her sexuality had completely taken her over, and she was helpless and desperate in her need to be fucked.

So desperate, so helpless, that she wasn't sure she could trust herself not to disobey her new Master's orders.

But did she *want* to obey Alfred's orders?

"Actually...just take me home," she said nervously to Phil. "It's a little out of your way, I think. Do you mind?"

"Not at all," said Phil, letting his eyes linger just a little bit on Monique as he glanced over at her.

As Phil drove Monique home, her discomfort mounted. She tried to think about that disgusting man in the park, since that seemed to eliminate her feelings of desire. But even the disgust she felt remembering that unfortunate incident couldn't drown out the over-whelming attraction she was feeling to Phil. Monique felt like if Phil had made a pass at her, she would have fucked him right there in the leather backseat of his Jag.

Monique felt guilty about that—she just *couldn't* disobey her new Master—not so soon after she'd found him! And Alfred had implied, if not outright stated, that the only way she was going to get fucked was to be a good slave and follow every order that was given to her. The first and most important was that she mustn't let another man have her. Not, at least, until Pietre gave her permission. Which, if it happened, would no doubt be after—maybe long after—Pietre had taken Monique for the first time.

Thinking about that, Monique was visited again with a sudden, vivid image of Pietre mounting her, climbing on top of her and pushing his cock inside her while she lay under him, panting and moaning, bound and captive, tied naked to his bed, while Alfred watched and chuckled with satisfaction. Monique could feel the ache, the tingle, flowing through her body; she tried to take a deep breath and relax, but when she did, all she could smell was Phil's sexy, musky cologne and the sharp male tang of his sweat.

Monique shuddered.

"Turn right here," she muttered, resisting the powerful urge to direct Phil to turn into that old empty cul-de-sac at the edge of the hill, to ask him to park the car and fuck her silly.

No, she couldn't! Monique told herself that she had to follow orders, had to obey Alfred's command, for Alfred's orders were as good as Pietre's. And Monique knew she would never get fucked by Pietre if she didn't do as she was told.

Then again, she was so horny she couldn't see straight—and this Phil was, without a doubt, very attractive. Monique could just casually invite him to drive somewhere secluded with her and park...and then she wouldn't *have* to wait until Pietre saw fit to fuck her. She could give it up right here, fucked from behind by this good-looking guy. She wouldn't mind at all losing it to Phil—right now, tonight, before the sun even went down—

"Which house is it?" asked Phil, as Monique realized they were right in front of her house.

"The yellow one," she told Phil reluctantly, wishing she could make the drive last forever, could let this exquisite torture go on until she couldn't stand it anymore and she threw herself on Phil and fucked him cross-eyed.

"Here we are," he said. "Can I walk you to your door?"

"You better not," blurted Monique, simply knowing that if he walked her to the front door, she was going to screw him right there on that stupid porch swing Dad had put in last summer.

"It was nice meeting you," said Phil. "I'm really sorry about that guy—"

"Thanks," said Monique, feigning a look of emotional trauma to hide her pain at parting with Phil without laying him.

"You know, Monique, I would...I would really like to see you some time—just to get a drink, or coffee or something..."

Oh God, thought Monique, a warmth spreading up to her belly, down across her thighs. She felt her nipples hardening as Phil spoke.

"Not to, you know, not that it has to mean anything, I would just like to—"

"I would like that," said Monique hoarsely. "I would really really like that. A lot. Really." She shifted uncomfortably in the leather seat, well aware of the fact that her nipples had hardened so fully that they must be quite visible to Phil's hungry eyes. They jutted through the dress, almost threatening to poke through the thin, sweat-damp material. "Really," Monique blurted, barely aware of what she was doing. "I would really really like it. Really."

Phil looked at her as though she was insane.

Damn, she thought to herself. *Too many really's.*

Phil slipped a business card out of his pocket and handed it to Monique. Without anywhere to put it, Monique clutched the business card in her hand, where it quickly got soaked with her sweat.

"Thanks," she said. "And thanks again for the ride."

"No problem," Phil said, nervously, looking a little uncomfortable.

He's probably wondering why I'm not getting out of the car, thought Monique, but no matter how she commanded her limbs to move, she just couldn't step out of the car.

Suddenly she lunged forward, as if she had no control

of her body whatsoever. She pressed her lips to Phil's, letting her tongue trail a path along his upper lip as she whimpered a little in the pleasure of the kiss. The brief, quick kiss seemed to last forever, and Monique felt her body responding intensely. She suddenly felt a wave of remorse and pulled back, her breast heaving as she panted with excitement.

"I'm sorry," she mumbled, fumbling for the door handle.

Phil gasped, "Wait—" as Monique almost fell out of the car.

Ignoring him, Monique slammed the door of the Jag and ran up the path to the house. She fumbled with her keys, acutely feeling the heat of Phil's gaze on her back, on her legs and ass, as he watched her from the car. But he didn't follow her, didn't try to stop her from running away from him, much as Monique wanted him to. By the time Monique got into the house, her knees were weak and she felt as though she was wet to the ankles.

Desperately, Monique slammed the door, locked and double-locked it. She heard the Jaguar pulling away. She peered through the peephole and saw that Phil had, indeed, left.

Monique breathed a sigh of relief. Then she realized she still had Phil's business card.

She looked at it, soaked with her sweat and crumpled in her hand.

Her relief gave way to a shiver that went through her body, and she looked through the peephole once more just to make sure Phil really had driven away. She felt a faint disappointment when she saw that he was, in fact, gone.

CHAPTER 11

Monique found a note taped to the refrigerator. Her parents had started their vacation. They'd gone off to their condo on the beach. They would be gone until the following Monday evening, Monique remembered. She realized with mixed fear and excitement that that meant she had the whole house to herself all week. She would be alone all weekend, and each evening next week. She was already incredibly hot and bothered from her intense flirt with Phil—could she manage to spend a whole weekend by herself without getting herself off?

And what of the coming week? Surely, Monique was doomed.

Monique had her doubts—she'd never managed to do that before. Not since she'd started masturbating and fantasizing, at least.

But Alfred had been very clear in his orders: She was not to climax. Monique could already feel the ache starting in her pussy—the ache of unrequited lust. Now that she was out of Phil's presence, Monique so wanted to take off all her clothes, lie back and fantasize about him mounting her, fucking her roughly—taking her. But she just couldn't do that, could she?

Monique sat down on the living room couch and turned on the TV. She found a public television channel showing a nature so—something totally innocuous. *There*, she thought. *At least this won't get me any hornier.* She tried to focus on the show, but her mind kept wandering to Phil, to Alfred, to Pietre. To the men in the park who had crowded around to help her. They had been so concerned for her well-being, but that hadn't stopped them from looking at her body like that. If they had known how desperately she needed to be fucked, would their concern for her have extended to satisfying that burning need inside her?

Yes, thought Monique, her hands drifting down the front of her body. *All of them…every last one of them…one after the other…*

She imagined them mounting her, taking her. Trying to satisfy her with hard cocks inside her cunt, ass, and mouth. But with every cock she took, she wanted more.

With each time they came inside her, Monique wanted another to do the same. Now Monique was leaning back in the leather couch, smelling the familiar, warm, comforting smell of that couch, watching as the Tiger-spotted Carnivorous Marmot stalked its prey. She tried desperately not to let her hands stray between her legs; she spread her thighs wide, so that she could not rub her thighs together, as she desperately wanted to do. But this meant that she could feel the cool air of the air-conditioning on her pussy, her aching pussy, the virgin pussy that so desperately needed to be fucked by dozens of cocks, one after the other—

Monique looked down at her body; the dress was soaked with sweat, and her nipples were quite evident under the fabric. Monique remembered Phil looking at her, his eyes devouring her nipples; she wondered if he'd been thinking about the way he wanted to take them into his mouth, suckle on them, bite them—

Now there was a naturalist on-camera—he was a young, virile-looking man with an Australian accent—he was incredibly cute, and had great muscles—he was wearing a tight T-shirt and threatened to bust out of his safari jacket—she wondered if he, too, would be willing to fuck her if she begged him to do so—

Unable to stop herself, Monique found her hands on her breasts, teasing and kneading them, pinching the nipples through the thin dress. She moaned softly in pleasure as she did so.

I shouldn't be doing this, she thought. *This is wrong. If I keep doing this, I'm going to have to make myself come. Then I'll be disobeying Alfred. Disobeying Pietre.* Thinking about how she was disobeying them only made images of her punishment come to mind. Perhaps they would make her lift her skirt and bend over to receive a flogging on her ass. Or on her breasts.

Moaning uncontrollably, Monique worked her nipples with each thumb and forefinger. She pinched harder, rolling her firm pink buds rhythmically. *It's okay*, thought Monique. *It's okay. As long as I don't touch my pussy. As long as I don't touch my clit.*

She kept her legs spread wide, leaning forward a little to get herself out of the position she was in. Lying back like that, with her legs spread so wide, all she could think about was how she was in the perfect position to get fucked. And with that short skirt, there wouldn't have been anything between the man in question and Monique. "God, that would be so good," moaned Monique to herself, out loud. "Getting fucked like that…just getting fucked…oh yes…."

Monique often talked to herself when she was masturbating. But she was rarely alone in the house, so she usually couldn't moan like that, couldn't cry out in her pleasure. Now, with nobody else in the whole place, Monique was wailing, moaning, thrashing her body about on the couch and rocking back and forth as she imagined—

Then Monique realized with horror that she felt like she was going to come.

How could that be? She hadn't even touched her pussy or her clit. All she was doing was rubbing her nipples! She must be mistaken...maybe it was just her imagination....

Monique went on pinching and rubbing her tits, feeling her pleasure mount.

She had incredibly sensitive nipples, but she'd never come just from pinching them—without touching her pussy or clit.

Monique stopped, her hands frozen on her tits. She was right on the edge.

She had heard about women who could come just from having their nipples stimulated. But she'd never done it to herself...then again, she'd never tried....

Whimpering, Monique jumped up from the couch, forcing herself to put her hands on her sides. She was so close to orgasm that the slightest sensation might set her off, might make her come in shuddering waves.

She couldn't disobey Pietre... she mustn't....

A cold shower, Monique decided. That was what she needed.

Better yet, a cold plunge.

Monique rushed out to the backyard, where there was a thirty-foot pool, her father's pride and joy. The fence technically wasn't really high enough for her to skinny-dip, but she did it sometimes anyway. The sun wasn't down yet, so it was possible that people from the surrounding houses might be able to see her—but at the moment, Monique feared that if she took the time to get her suit, she would find herself rubbing her pussy until she came.

Monique swept her dress off in a single movement and dove gracefully into the water. The water wasn't bad—not quite cold enough to cool her down. But then, with the way Monique was feeling, she would have melted a pool full of ice water and probably boiled it off. She swam around, feeling the cool water on her body, enjoying the way it felt on her bare pussy. It was amazing how different, how exposed, she felt now that she didn't have any hair down there. Shaving it off like that had been such a delicious idea...but now, every time she felt the wind on her bare snatch or felt the water on it...like now....

Monique tried to work off her sexual need by doing some laps. But the increase in her heart rate felt too much like sex, and soon she was fantasizing that Pietre was forcing her to do laps, ordering her to work out in order to tone her body for him. That just made her hornier, and every stroke she took made her want sex even more.

Finally, Monique crawled, panting and desperate, out of the water. She made her way to the chaise lounge and lay there nude, loving the feel of the setting sun on her body.

Monique let her hands linger over her breasts again, feeling how the sensations of her fingertips brushing her nipples mingled with the warmth of the slanted sunlight. She began to tease her nipples again, finding them quite firm.

God, it felt so good...she wouldn't come. She just couldn't come from playing with her nipples, could she? She'd never done it before....

Monique began pinching, rubbing them, and soon she was moaning again, mounting the crest toward orgasm.

She would just play a little, then. She wouldn't make herself come.

Monique played with her tits hungrily, feeling the lust grow in her body. She rocked back and forth on the chaise lounge, her eyes closed, her breath coming short.

When her eyes fluttered open, Monique gasped. She had never noticed that wide crack in the fence before! A plank was missing—

And framed in the spot where the plank should have been—watching her with wide eyes and obvious interest—was Hank, the guy she'd stripped for just last night!

Monique felt a wave of fear. Maybe he was going to come in. Climb the fence and come over here and fuck her.

That's right, fuck her. Fuck her right here on the

chaise lounge by the pool. Fuck her hot pussy for the first time, make her come—

Watching Monique intently, but without saying a word, Hank reached down and pulled down the gym shorts he wore and took out his dick.

Monique was a lot closer to it than she'd been last night—and so she could see just how big it really was. It was just enormous—and seeing it made her want to crawl over there, get to her knees before Hank, and take his cock into her mouth as he leaned up against the fence, sticking his dick through the hole in the fence—

Hank wrapped his hand around his prick and began to jerk it rapidly, rhythmically pulling his pud.

Monique went back to squeezing her nipples, pinching them, rolling them in her fingers—

Matching her rhythm to Hank's.

Monique seemed to sense instinctively that Hank was going to come. Seeing him jerk his prick so fast made Monique wish she could be the one doing it—with her hand, her mouth, her pussy—

"Oh yes," she gasped, and she realized that she was straying dangerously close to her own orgasm. Just one little touch....

Monique's hand slid slowly down her body; her fingers worked into her slit, and Monique began to rub her clitoris—

Hank let out a loud groan, and Monique saw streams of his jizz shooting into the grass just as her own orgasm overtook her, exploding through her naked body. She thrashed on the chaise lounge, moaning in remorse even as she gave herself over to her approaching orgasm. Then Monique froze—she was on the very edge of her climax. She held still, willing herself not to come.

She had to lie there without moving—but soon, thankfully, she felt her orgasm dwindling. She looked up as she relaxed—Hank was gone. She was alone by the pool. But she had managed to avoid coming, painful as it was.

Monique blushed a deep red. Would she be in trouble if Pietre or Alfred found out about this? Alfred had told her to display her body to men. Didn't this count?

Monique supposed it sort of did. But she still felt acute guilt and fear of Alfred's anger. Perhaps Alfred and Pietre would punish her if they found out about her behavior.

When they find out about it, Monique thought ruefully, for something instinctively told her that even though there was no way they could know what had happened, somehow her new Masters knew everything about her....

CHAPTER 12

Monique awakened early on Saturday morning naked, tangled in sheets sweaty with her sweat and the smell of her sex, with her pussy already wet and her nipples hard from the erotic dreams she'd been having. It seemed as though her whole body was alive with new sensation, the fires of her sex stoked by the erotic tension of knowing she was wholly owned. She belonged to Pietre Salazar, and he was going to use her as she ought to be used, as a slut like her deserved to be used. Her pleasure was to be denied, and the dozen or so times she'd stroked herself to the very brink of orgasm had started an inferno inside her that was impossible for Monique to ignore. She ached for sex, yet she knew that it was to be denied her. She could not yet be fucked. She would have to earn the right to feel a man's flesh pushing inside her, taking her, possessing her. She would remain a virgin until she had proven her worthiness. Pietre had ordered it thus.

The very thought sent shivers through Monique. Pietre was going to fuck her one day. When he'd properly trained her. When he'd satisfied himself that Monique was a suitable slave, Pietre was going to use Monique endlessly.

And the using had begun already. She was to dress in the manner Pietre had instructed. She was to show her body off to whomever wanted to see it. She was to wear the most revealing clothes possible. No panties. Only a G-string. Her bra must leave her nipples visible. Her neckline could not come higher than her nipples, so her cleavage would always be evident. She was to wear a garter belt and stockings—with the G-string on the outside, so it could be taken off and she could be fucked without removing the garters. She was to wear skirts that ended no more than eight inches above her knee.

In short, she was to dress like a slut.

Despite her horror, Monique was almost delirious with happiness. She had always wanted to be a shameless exhibitionist—now she was being forced to do exactly that. And as she thought about all the men who would look at her ass and legs and breasts, one phrase repeated itself endlessly.

Unlimited credit

On the verge of orgasm already, Monique jumped out of bed and raced for the shower.

While Monique was in the shower, she remembered that Alfred had ordered her to shave every day except Sunday. Surely one day wouldn't be a problem? But Monique felt the acute fear of being punished that aroused such deep pleasure inside her, and she knew that she should obey Alfred's orders to the letter. So she shaved her pussy, careful not to be too rough. Even so, she felt a little irritated, and looked forward to going to that store—PleasureLand—and getting whatever lotion it was that would help alleviate the discomfort.

Monique wasn't sure what she ought to wear, so she finally decided on her pencil skirt. But she couldn't wear it as-is—she would have to fold it up. She did so, careful to make sure that the skirt ended eight inches above her knee. She wanted to go without anything underneath it, but she knew she would be expected to wear underwear when trying on lingerie. So she dug the G-string out from under her mattress. It wasn't in the best condition, since she had never washed it after her long prom night of lust. Monique sniffed at it distastefully. But there wasn't anything else for her to wear that would fulfill Alfred's orders.

So Monique slipped the dirty G-string on, feeling more than a little sleazy, but somewhat excited by that.

Now Monique had the problem of what to wear on her top half. Alfred had been very clear that she shouldn't wear anything that concealed her breasts. And if she wore a bra—a real bra—she had to wear it a cup size too small! Since Monique's breasts were just a bit too big for a C-cup, a B would leave them hanging out everywhere. Even Monique, who knew she was rapidly becoming a shameless exhibitionist, was horrified by that thought.

But she knew better than to disobey Alfred. She could go without any bra at all—but what if she was seen changing in one of the dressing rooms? Wouldn't the salesgirls think that odd? After all, a woman with breasts as large as Monique's rarely went around without a bra. But all her bras were C-cups. And she certainly didn't have a demi-bra or push-up bra of any sort. She did have the one deliciously too small she'd inherited from Katrina, her older sister—but that bra's label claimed it was a C-cup, though Monique knew from experience that it most certainly was not a C-cup.

Even so, she would be breaking the letter of Alfred's law. And she couldn't bring herself to do that—not just yet.

Then Monique remembered—her mother was a B-cup.

That seemed so deviant, so naughty—to borrow one of Mom's brassieres so she could go about in a cup-size much too small for her because her lover and Master had ordered her to show herself off. But it also excited her, and soon Monique found herself digging through Mom's drawers—finally finding a black lace bra that would do the trick nicely. Monique felt restrained and revealed as her breasts popped out over the top of the lace bra, and her nipples were hard momentarily. But after she'd put on her favorite tight sweater, she looked herself over in the full-length mirror and decided that she looked just wonderful. Luckily the sweater was rather low-cut, so with a little creative tugging, Monique could make the neckline low enough to meet Alfred's cleavage rule.

Monique put on her black shoes with their four-inch-high heels, and she was ready to go shopping—to make a whore of herself on Pietre's money. She was so excited she almost succumbed to her sudden desire for a brief pre-shopping-trip wank.

Mom and Dad had been driven to the airport by a friend, so Dad's Jaguar was in the driveway and the keys hung from the bulletin board. Monique had been instructed not to drive the Jag, but she just couldn't resist. Besides, she would look so elegant pulling into the Garrison mall, a rather upscale establishment.

So Monique took the Jag, and felt her body temperature rising as she neared the stores where she could repeat that delicious phrase over and over in her mind.

Unlimited credit

She was getting wet already.

† † †

Monique walked into PleasureLand and felt immediately embarrassed. Despite her sexual excitement, it dismayed her to see so many representations of genitalia displayed so openly.

Still, it was sort of a turn-on. And the place was shockingly clean—not smelling of bleach the way Monique had always heard that porno shops were. It was clean, well-lit, and rather comfortable. Three-quarters of the people in the store were women, and it was doing quite a brisk business. It wasn't even 11:00 in the morning yet.

PleasureLand sold a wide variety of toys and books. A sign off to one side indicated a door leading to another room where the lingerie was sold. But in the main room, Monique was particularly shocked by two things. First was the wall full of dildos, which immediately sent a shiver through her body and made her pussy feel warm. There must have been a hundred dildos of all sizes, shapes, and colors, jutting out of the wall as if they were all just begging Monique to lift her skirt, wriggle her ass back and impale herself on them. One after the other. She would need a stepladder for most of them....

Then there were the floor-to-ceiling photographs of pussies.

Monique almost yelped when she saw those. Not that she was disturbed by female genitalia—far from it.

230

In fact, she loved to look at her own genitals in a hand-mirror—though she never would have admitted that to anyone, possibly not even to Pietre or Alfred. And certainly not to Miss Pynchon, who, Monique suspected, probably *never* looked at her own pussy, and really ought to do so from time to time.

But other women's pussies frightened her a little. Miss Pynchon's had certainly terrified her even though she hadn't even really gotten a look at it—and that was a special case, Monique felt.

And seeing a pussy floor-to-ceiling was a bit much even for the increasingly exhibitionistic Monique.

Monique was struck by a thought then—did Pietre have other lovers? Would he expect her to go to bed with both of them? Once he had taken her, of course. Monique's warmth, and her fear, grew as she thought about that. Clearly Pietre did have other lovers, since Alfred had told her that the salesgirls would be quite familiar with Pietre's lovers, and would know how to handle Monique once she told them that.

But Monique was terrified that she might be expected to make love with another woman for Pietre's enjoyment. Certainly she had read of such things in her shoplifted paperbacks, but was it possible he would really expect that of her? Expect her to kiss a woman, touch her, make love with her—all so that Pietre could watch and enjoy the spectacle?

Monique's fear overwhelmed her, but she had to

231

admit there was a certain excitement to that fear. She knew that she must do anything Pietre demanded of her—*anything*. But—*that?*

"May I help you, Miss?" Monique realized she was standing there foolishly looking at the image of a vagina twice as tall as she was. So she turned and looked stupidly at a beautiful girl about her age, perhaps slightly older. Monique sought for something to say, and couldn't find anything. The girl really was very beautiful, wasn't she? She had bright green eyes not unlike Monique's, and lovely blonde hair cut in a bob. She wasn't wearing much more than Monique—a little less, in fact. Just a mini-dress, low-cut in the front and quite short. The woman had fantastic legs, long and smooth and firm. The dress was tight on top, so Monique could see that the woman's breasts were not at all large, not nearly as large as Monique's own. Perhaps just an A-cup, then, not quite enough for a B. She had full, very kissable lips. The woman was several inches taller than Monique, and her body was quite entrancing. Monique found herself wondering wickedly if this woman's pussy looked like the photograph on the wall.

"Like the photograph?" asked the young woman.

Monique searched desperately for an answer. "I...yes, I like it very much."

"It's mine," the woman smiled.

"Oh," said Monique uncomfortably. "You're a photographer?"

The woman giggled. "No, I mean the pussy. I'm the model."

Monique blushed. "Oh, I was just wondering..." she blurted out, and stopped herself. "It's quite lovely."

The woman winked lasciviously. "If you play your cards right, perhaps you can see it up close some time soon." The woman's eyes flickered over Monique's revealed body, and Monique felt as though the woman was looking directly through her tight clothing, stripping her naked in front of all these people.

Monique's heart pounded in her ears. The woman licked her lips as she looked Monique over. Monique felt her breath coming short—she felt about ready to faint. But her nipples were hardening suddenly, and she could feel herself getting wet under the short skirt.

"I'm just teasing," said Brianna, the seductive look in her eyes telling Monique that she was definitely not just teasing. "But it really is me. I'm the model."

"Oh, that's wonderful," said Monique, getting her breath back.

"I know the photographer. She likes to take pictures of ordinary women—you know, not models. She would probably even take a picture of you if you were interested. I mean, like this. She doesn't do faces so much. Though you really are quite beautiful."

The woman said it casually, so that it didn't appear to be a come-on. But Monique was still having a hard time keeping her mind on the conversation. She was thinking about that pussy on the wall, and how it belonged to this rather striking young woman in front of her. And how that woman, no matter how much she claimed that she was just teasing Monique, had just made a blatant come-on to her.

Monique was horrified—she had never responded this strongly to another woman. Well, except for Miss Pynchon.

But she couldn't. She simply couldn't let herself be seduced into a flirtation with this young woman.

"I'm here to see Brianna," said Monique nervously. "Is she here?"

"Pietre sent you," said the woman smoothly, smiling. "You're one of his women. Aren't you?"

Monique was now blushing terribly. She nodded, her eyes dropping to the floor.

"Yes," said Monique. "I'm...I'm his."

"Ooooh, you say that with such submission. He's really done a job on you. Well, I'm Brianna. I'm pleased to be of service. What did he tell you? The usual?"

Monique felt more embarrassed than ever. So it was true. She was one of a long line of slave girls Pietre had sent here to be outfitted in slutty and revealing clothes, prepared for their deflowerment. She was nothing but a minor addition to his harem, and Brianna would see that she was properly clothed for Pietre to initiate her.

"I...I don't know," whispered Monique. "What's usual?"

"Why don't you tell me what he ordered for you?" said Brianna with a smile on her face, taking Monique's hand and leading her toward the lingerie room.

Monique was tangibly aroused to be among all this lace and satin. Brianna led Monique over into a corner and placed her in front of a three-way mirror. Monique realized that the other customers couldn't see them very well at all.

"Now, let's get a good look at you," Brianna said, coming up behind Monique, "while you tell me what Pietre has dictated for you." Brianna leaned very close, pressing her body against Monique's back and putting her hands on Monique's shoulders. Soon, before Monique knew it, Brianna was drawing her hands forward, down onto Monique's breasts. Monique almost jumped to be touched like that by a woman, but she felt her resolve melting at Brianna's touch.

Alfred had ordered that men couldn't touch her. Did that include women?

Obviously not, since Brianna was familiar with Pietre's demands, and yet was touching Monique in public. Well, not quite in full view of the customers —but certainly if someone had wandered over, they would have seen Brianna touching Monique's breasts.

Monique was horrified at her quick response to Brianna's touch. The very last thing she wanted to do in the world was sleep with a woman—surely that would

be going against Alfred's orders! But he had only said
that "men" couldn't touch her. So perhaps—

But the idea was unpleasant to Monique. Well, not
wholly unpleasant. But she knew she couldn't do it. And
yet her nipples felt hard as Brianna began to pinch them.

"Hold still," Brianna whispered, and Monique fought
to obey her. Brianna continued to knead Monique's
breasts, teasing her nipples to full hardness as she
kissed the back of Monique's neck.

"Surely these are quite lovely," whispered Brianna,
her breath warm and gentle in Monique's ear. "I wish I
had more, myself. But I'll not begrudge you how
wonderful yours are. Certainly Pietre wants you to
show them off quite shamelessly, doesn't he? Doesn't
he, Monique?"

Brianna had known her name without Monique
telling it to her. Clearly this had all been set up by Pietre
and Alfred. Monique was helpless in Brianna's hands.

Monique nodded, unable to stop herself from moaning softly as Brianna pinched her nipples harder.

"Please," she heard herself gasping. "Please stop."

"Tell me what he ordered you to do," said Brianna.
"Tell me how he wants you to show off these lovely
breasts of yours."

"I...I really should wear a D-cup," Monique heard
herself confessing. "He wants me to wear a B. When I'm
not wearing a push-up or a demi-bra."

"Mmmm," sighed Brianna, kissing Monique's ear.

"That will leave these tits of yours spilling out every-where. But you'll like that, won't you?"

Monique nodded. She couldn't believe she'd just confessed that to this stranger. But surely if Pietre had sent her here, he meant for her to surrender utterly to the pleasures of the shop.

"And what else? These legs of yours..." Brianna slid her hand down Monique's belly, past the hem of the skirt. She stroked Monique's inner thigh. "They're deli-cious. He wants you to show them off, doesn't he?"

Monique nodded, listening to the sound of her own breath. She was getting incredibly wet, despite her dismay at responding this sexually to another woman. Was Brianna seducing her?

"Tell me how he wants you to show your legs off," said Brianna.

"My skirts can't be more than eight inches above the knee," moaned Monique softly.

"Ooooh, you've gotten off easily," said Brianna, stroking Monique's inner thigh. "Mine are twelve inches. But sometimes I like to wear them shorter. And I am quite a bit taller than you."

Monique could feel Brianna's own small, firm breasts pressing against her back. The nipples were quite hard.

She felt Brianna's hand sliding up her inner thigh, toward her pussy.

"This wet little snatch of yours," Brianna breathed, nibbling at Monique's ear. "It is wet, isn't it?"

Monique shivered, unable to answer.

Then she felt Brianna's hand sliding down into her G-string—Brianna was going to find out for herself.

Right here in public.

"What if someone sees us?" whimpered Monique desperately.

"Then they'll know what a perfect slut you are," sighed Brianna as she slid her hand deeper into Monique's G-string. She teased, not yet dipping down into Monique's pussy to find out how wet she was.

"You're shaved smooth," said Brianna. "He's ordered you to do that?"

"I...I did it on my own," said Monique uncomfortably as Brianna stroked her hairless crotch. "But now he's ordered me to do it every day except Sunday."

Brianna kissed Monique's ear. "Then you'll need some lotion," she said. "He told you to get some, didn't he?"

Monique nodded. Brianna's fingers continued downward.

"He lets you wear a G-string," cooed Brianna. "You're quite lucky. Some of his girls go about with nothing on at all. But you're supposed to wear garters and stockings, aren't you?"

Monique nodded quickly.

"You were careless this morning, weren't you?"

Monique nodded again.

Brianna sighed. "Oh, you'll be punished severely for that. When I tell him. He'll take forever to fuck you if you keep this up. Is it true you're a virgin? Never been fucked?"

Monique nodded sadly.

"Never even been to bed with a girl?"

Monique whispered, "Never."

"But you're wet right now, aren't you? Don't you wish you could get fucked right now?"

Monique shivered with arousal, but couldn't bring herself to admit to Brianna how hot and wet she really was. Slowly, Brianna slipped her finger down into Monique's slit, stroking between her lips and feeling how slick and juicy her pussy had gotten.

"Oh, you're just dripping," said Brianna teasingly. "Good thing he lets you wear a G-string, or I'd have to have the carpet cleaned."

Brianna began to tease and stroke Monique's clitoris, which had gotten quite erect and ached from her arousal. Monique let out a louder moan.

"Shhhh! We don't want to alert every man in the store that there's a tight wet virgin here just begging to be fucked—or do we?"

Between the feeling of Brianna's finger on her clit and the gentle squeeze of Brianna's hand on her nipple, Monique was ready to come. That couldn't happen—Alfred had ordered her not to climax! She couldn't go against his orders so soon—it would be a disaster! But Brianna seemed to anticipate this, and she sighed. "He's ordered you not to come, hasn't he?"

Monique nodded thankfully.

Brianna's hand slid out of Monique's G-string and Monique felt a tangible sense of relief. Her tension remained though—she was still very close to orgasm. She glanced around—no one seemed to be looking, and they were still fairly well concealed.

Brianna's fingers, slick with Monique's juices, traveled up Monique's body. Brianna gently parted Monique's lips with her middle finger.

Monique felt a wave of revulsion, but with it there was an accompanying surge of arousal. She accepted Brianna's finger into her mouth, tasting the rich sharpness of her own juices. She licked Brianna's fingers clean, and Brianna gave her a gentle kiss on the lips. Her tongue just barely grazed Monique's lower lip, which was tangy with her fluids.

"Now let's get you some clothes," she sighed. "You'll need a new G-string, at least."

Brianna led Monique through the shop, taking great delight in picking out a wide variety of undergarments for Monique. She selected a dozen G-strings, at least that many bras, mostly push-ups and demi-bras. Then there were a couple of full brassieres—of thin material and in B-cup, of course. Monique could feel her breasts spilling out everywhere over the lace top of Mom's B-cup bra—she thought what a slut she'd look like always wearing such skimpy undergarments.

The thought excited her.

Brianna also selected a couple of camisoles of very thin, see-through material, and a variety of garter belts and stockings. Finally, she led Monique into a large dressing room and closed the door.

"Well, now," said Brianna, sitting in the dressing room's only chair. "I'm going to enjoy this."

Monique blushed a deep, hot red. "Aren't you going to…?"

"I'm going to sit right here," said Brianna with a smile on her pretty face. "While you undress and try on each one of those outfits for me. Every last one."

"I can't—I can't just undress in front of you…"

"Oh, certainly you can," smiled Brianna, her legs parting just enough to reveal that she wasn't wearing anything under that short dress. No panties or G-string —just stockings affixed to a garter belt. Was she one of the women that Pietre ordered to go without panties?

"You should get used to it," said Brianna, tugging her dress up further to show the lace tops of her stockings. "He'll have you shown off to everyone he fancies. Don't become prudish now."

Monique felt a wave of heat going through her body.

Mechanically, she began to undress.

Once she'd taken off her clothes and unhitched her bra, she reached to select the elements of the first outfit.

"Wait," said Brianna, her voice low and seductive. "That's not everything."

"But I'm supposed to wear underpants when I..." Monique began.

"Perhaps in a conventional store," sighed Brianna. "Here, you'll try on your new clothes as they are meant to be worn."

Monique looked at Brianna in horror. Of course, the woman had just touched her pussy—and what an intense pleasure that had been, much as Monique would have liked to deny it. But she couldn't—nor could she deny the heat that was building in her pussy as she undressed before Brianna. As Brianna's eyes moved slowly over her breasts, over her ass, over her legs. Devouring her.

"Well," said Brianna. "You haven't got all day. You've still got Flirt! and Next to Nothing and Bonne Femme to visit—and then it's Chained Heat for you, little sex-slave."

Nervously, Monique took off her G-string and stood naked and revealed before Brianna. She was acutely aware of her pussy being shaved clean and unprotected, even by her faint sprinkling of pubic hair.

"Lovely," said Brianna, slowly lifting her dress to reveal her naked pussy. Brianna, too, was shaved.

Monique looked at Brianna's pussy in fascination, half wishing that she could touch it. Was Brianna as wet as she was?

"I'm wetter," said Brianna, seeming to read Monique's thoughts. "I'm gushing. You did quite a number on me out there, wriggling that pretty little ass of yours every time I touched you. Believe me, I'm even wetter than you are."

"Are…are you one of his women, too?" asked Monique stupidly.

"No questions," said Brianna. "Now start with the blue garter belt. G-string on the outside of the garters, remember—so he can pull it down and fuck your bare pussy any time he wants."

Monique went wet to the knees when she heard that phrase. She hurriedly began to put on the garter belt.

Monique became more and more aroused with each outfit she tried on for Brianna. Her pussy was getting unbelievably wet. If she didn't get off soon she was going to go mad with frustration.

But Monique knew she couldn't climax—couldn't disobey Alfred's orders that blatantly. Especially not with Brianna here.

But Brianna was touching herself. She was sliding her fingers up and down her wet slit while she gave Monique fashion advice.

"These crotchless panties are nice," moaned Brianna softly. "Then he can just lift your skirt and fuck you without any preliminaries. That's what he likes to do to his girls who don't wear any panties. Maybe you'll be one of them someday.

"Lovely bra, makes your tits look even bigger than

they are," she went on. "I imagine he'll want to slide his cock right between them. They're so lovely. He's such a fondness for well-built girls like you...I wish I had more of what you've got."

Monique wondered for the thousandth time if Brianna was one of Pietre's lovers. She could feel her pussy surging as she thought about the very pretty Brianna being fucked by Pietre's hard cock.

If she was a lover of Pietre's, did that also mean that Brianna got fucked by Alfred?

Despite stroking herself, Brianna didn't ever call out in orgasm. Monique was getting so desperate to see Brianna come, she almost forgot about her own agonizing arousal.

Finally, after a long, torturous foreplay, Monique tried on the last outfit—a red garter belt, G-string and red stockings, with a matching bustier that pushed her breasts up and out. Brianna stood up and quickly slipped her dress over her head. She stood there in nothing but white garter belt and stockings—no bra at all. Her firm breasts looked wonderful out of their thin cotton prison. Monique was shocked at how excited she was to see Brianna almost nude.

Before Monique knew what was happening, Brianna had put her arms around Monique and pushed her up against the flimsy wall of the cubicle. Monique gasped as Brianna grabbed Monique's knee and pulled it up roughly between her thighs, demandingly settling atop

Monique's knee as she ground against Monique's body.

Then Brianna was kissing Monique, and Monique forgot her shyness and even her disgust as she felt Brianna's supple tongue sliding between her lips, teasing her own tongue out. Brianna nipped at Monique's lower lip with her teeth, as Monique put her foot on the edge of the dressing room chair, holding her leg up between Brianna's legs. She left her hands at her sides, afraid to so much as touch Brianna. She couldn't be doing this. She couldn't be almost naked like this, pressed up against a woman she barely knew—against *any* woman—she had to be dreaming!

"That's right," moaned Brianna softly. "That's right—I'm going to come! Oh God, you're going to get fucked so good, my sweet little virgin—oh!"

Then Brianna's whole body was shuddering, her moans turned to whimpers, and the frightened Monique still did not reach up to touch those glorious, smooth, ivory-white breasts of Brianna's, did not touch those coral nipples, did not dip down to place her mouth on the hardness of those tits, much as she wanted to. Much as Monique desperately craved the taste and the feel of Brianna's lovely body, she was much too frightened to give in to her unexpected and unasked-for desires.

"You will," said Brianna in a whisper as she finished coming, once again giving Monique the uncanny feeling that the girl could read her thoughts. "You will give

245

in to all your desires, whether you want to or not. Your new master will see to that."

Brianna slid smoothly away from Monique, both their bodies sheened with sweat. Brianna reached out for her dress and quickly slipped it on over her head, then buttoned up and straightened it.

"Get dressed," said Brianna firmly. "There are other surprises waiting for you at the other stores. The lotion and a few other things will be waiting for you. Bring everything to the front counter and Holly will ring you up. Everything will be taken care of."

With that cryptic remark, Brianna slipped out of the dressing room, leaving a panting and very bewildered Monique pulsing mere inches from her orgasm, her pussy on fire with hunger. Monique stood there, feeling her pussy soak through the red satin G-string as she remembered what Brianna's body had felt like pressed against hers.

Monique desperately wished she could violate every one of the restrictions Alfred had placed on her sexuality.

Preferably all at once, without having to leave the dressing room.

Instead, she began to get dressed.

CHAPTER 13

Monique's day had been long and progressively more perplexing. She had gone from PleasureLand to Flirt!. There at Flirt!, she had asked for Chelsea, as Alfred had instructed her. Chelsea, also not much older than Monique, was a striking girl with blonde hair which she kept in pigtails, for a wonderfully deviant effect. She was quite fetching, and Monique found herself looking taking great notice of Chelsea's large, firm breasts under her tight top. After the experience with Brianna, Monique was hopelessly confused—she knew she wasn't interested in women, but if that was so then why couldn't she take her eyes off of Chelsea's nipples as they hardened under her gaze.

247

She really oughtn't to be wearing a top like that, Monique found herself thinking. Not that she was complaining, really, but it didn't seem advisable. It was a V-necked athletic shirt with a big number across the front—and it was pretty evident that Chelsea wasn't wearing much underneath. If anything.

Chelsea, too, was expecting Monique, and asked her how it had gone at PleasureLand.

"Oh, you know," murmured Monique, nervous about everyone knowing where she'd been. "The usual."

"I bet," said Chelsea with a lascivious wink. She took Monique's hand and led her through the store. "I know just what Pietre has in mind for you. Did he order you to go without panties?"

Monique was blushing a deep red, her eyes unwillingly locked on Chelsea's pretty ass in her tight skirt.

"No," she finally said. "I'm to wear a G-string. Or crotchless panties."

"Ooooh, lucky girl. Are you shaving down there?"

"Yes," Monique breathed, knowing that she should be offended by this casual talk about her sexual proclivities—but knowing, as well, that she had surrendered control, utterly, to Pietre. And, through him, to this Chelsea woman.

And besides. Monique could feel herself getting wet all over again as Chelsea questioned her.

"Then let's get you dressed up in something really, really cute. He's going to want your skirts short, isn't he?"

"Eight inches above the knee," Monique answered without thinking.

Chelsea giggled. "I'm sure he'll raise that hemline as you go along. He likes it short enough to pull up without any effort. You know why?" She giggled some more. Looking Monique up and down with eyes that gave away the obvious sexual excitement she was feeling.

Well, this Chelsea certainly was a flirt.

Monique hadn't expected it to happen. She would have avoided it if she could have. But how could she defy Chelsea, who was obviously doing Alfred's bidding?

Chelsea helped Monique pick out a wide variety of short skirts, low-cut tops, and a few pairs of tight, low-slung pants in "exotic materials"—PVC and plastic. Then Chelsea led Monique into one of the dressing rooms.

Like PleasureLand, Flirt! had private dressing rooms with big mirrors. There was one chair, and Chelsea used it to sit in as she told Monique to undress.

This time, Monique was excited by the prospect of undressing in front of the salesgirl. She felt almost as if she was undressing in front of Pietre.

Perhaps that explained why she got so wet when she felt Chelsea's eyes on her naked body, and why her arousal mounted with each new outfit she tried on for Chelsea's approving eyes. More than once, Chelsea giggled and clapped her hands when Monique put on a

particularly revealing dress or tight pants. Soon, Chelsea
had found other ways to make her approval plain.

Monique could feel how wet her pussy was already.
When Chelsea snugged up her short skirt, Monique
thought she would simply die of excitement.

Even so, she didn't dare get close to Chelsea. One
touch on her clit might send her over the edge.

"Don't worry," sighed Chelsea, once again seeming to
read Monique's mind. "I won't make you come. I know
he's ordered you not to. Hasn't he?"

Monique nodded quickly, looking with fascination
as Chelsea revealed that she wasn't wearing any panties
under her skirt. And her pussy, like Monique's, and like
Brianna's, was shaved.

Except Chelsea's pussy was also pierced. Three rings
through each side, and one through her clitoris.

Monique gasped when she realized that.

"I was a bad girl," sighed Chelsea seductively as she
began to rub her pierced clit. "I let my ex-boyfriend fuck
me. Two of them, actually. Alfred found out about it."

So Chelsea was one of Pietre's slaves. Monique felt a
surge of excitement at the knowledge.

"How did he find out about it?" asked Monique
nervously.

"Oh, he has lots of ways of finding things out,"
giggled Chelsea, with a nasty, mischievous smile on her
face. "You'll learn all about them. After he found out,
Alfred ordered my pussy pierced so he could fasten it

shut." Chelsea giggled as she began to stroke her clit faster. "But I just let my ex-boyfriend fuck me in the ass. Alfred found out about that. So he took care of that part, too." Chelsea laughed as she arched her back, lifting her ass off the chair.

Monique didn't even want to think about how Alfred had taken care of preventing Chelsea from having anal sex.

"You'll find out," sighed Chelsea, as if she knew exactly what Monique was thinking. "You'll learn all the things he can do to control you. You'll learn not to fight them. You'll learn to love them. The point is, soon I learned my lesson. It took a while, but now I do exactly what Alfred tells me to do. And I like it that way—oh!"

Chelsea was nearing her climax, shuddering as she pumped her hips up and down. Monique watched with fascination as Chelsea began to climax.

"You'll learn," gasped Chelsea as she came. "You'll learn all his tricks. Oh!"

Chelsea sank onto the chair, her eyes fixed on Monique's body.

Then Chelsea giggled again.

"Come on, Monique. You know you want to. Just touch yourself a little. He'll never know. At least, I won't tell him."

That was all Monique could stand. She moaned softly as she felt her hands pulling up her skirt.

"No," she gasped. "I can't!"

"Just one little tiny orgasm," panted Chelsea. "Come sit in my lap while you do it. He'll never find out. You deserve it. Buying all these clothes to please him. Just make yourself come once. Better yet, let me do it. Please? I just want to touch that yummy pussy of yours."

It was as though Monique tried to give her body orders, but she couldn't get it to obey. She walked over to where Chelsea sat, eagerly frigging her wet pussy with her fingers.

"Are you really a virgin?" asked Chelsea nastily. "Really never been fucked? By a man or a woman?"

Monique nodded as she lifted off the dress she'd been trying on. No, she couldn't be doing this. She couldn't. She simply couldn't do this.

Then Monique was taking off the G-string, and in another second the too-tight bra was off. Nude except for her high-heeled shoes, Monique came closer to Chelsea, who was fucking her own pussy with two fingers.

"Come on," Chelsea gasped, putting her legs together to give Monique a place to sit. "Let me do it. I'm good at it—Pietre will tell you how good I am at it."

No, she couldn't be doing this. Couldn't. Shouldn't.

Monique's mind protested, even as she sat in Chelsea's lap.

Then she felt Chelsea's arms around her as she spread her legs, leaning back against the surprisingly strong girl. Chelsea began kissing Monique's neck as

Monique felt Chelsea's hands creeping over her body. With her left hand, Chelsea took hold of Monique's breasts, squeezing and kneading them as she teased the nipples.

"Oooh, they're nice and big," she cooed. "He likes that."

Chelsea slid her right hand between Monique's legs, her fingers working skillfully up and down Monique's juicing slit. Monique let out an uncontrolled moan as she felt Chelsea's fingertips on her clit. The rapid, circular motions drove Monique into a frenzy almost immediately—she could feel herself reaching the crest in an instant, closing in on her own intense orgasm.

"He'll pierce you here, too," giggled Chelsea, "When he finds out about this. When I tell him."

Chelsea had gauged her timing perfectly. With that, Monique climaxed with a groan, squirming in Chelsea's lap. Unable to stop herself. Unable to stop the pleasure which exploded through her. Unable to prevent herself from being swept away on the tide of ecstasy—knowing full well that she was breaking Alfred's commandment.

Tearfully, as Monique finished, she gasped out desperately, "You won't really tell him, will you?"

"Of course I will," sighed Chelsea, kissing Monique tenderly on the lips. "Just kidding!"

Then Chelsea giggled evilly.

Chapter 14

Somewhere in her heart, Monique knew would be performing a different form of worship that Sunday morning.

She was awakened early by the doorbell. Monique lay in bed, deliciously naked, tangled up among her sweat-smelling covers, having an intensely erotic dream about being enslaved and repeatedly fucked by a rugby team. The doorbell rang over and over again.

Monique had gone to bed wearing one of the skimpy silk negligees from Next to Nothing—something wonderfully naughty and slutty. Of course she'd ended up squirming out of it and masturbating before she went to sleep—several times, in fact, since each time she stopped short of orgasm and had to lie there very still for a long time before relaxing. It was so difficult to go to sleep in that state!

But the dream about the rugby team had served as an ample reward, seemingly lasting most of the night.

Monique finally managed to pull herself out of her erotic reveries and stumble out of bed. Who could be coming by this early?

Monique was so disoriented that she almost rushed down half-naked to answer the door. In fact, Monique was already quite used to being naked and half-clothed in the delicious garments she had purchased on her Master's account.

She had been a very bad girl all Saturday—without ever quite breaking Alfred's order against orgasm or contact with a man.

Except that one time, with Chelsea.

And Monique wondered if Chelsea had just been teasing her when she'd said she was going to tell Alfred about the orgasm.

It appeared that the little slut had not been teasing at all.

Now, as she fumbled for her short little satin robe, she felt the pain in her belly that told her she'd gone too far. Perhaps in more ways than one. She had read about "blue balls," which men got when they were aroused endlessly without getting off. Could she be getting the same sort of thing? Oh, but it had felt so good finally to come at Chelsea's hand—to feel Chelsea stroking her and getting her off. It had been so delicious Monique felt wet all over again just remembering it. And she knew it felt so good because she'd held off for so interminably long, coming close each time but never quite getting off.

Until Chelsea spoiled her perfect record.

The doorbell rang again and again. Monique finally made it to the door and flung it open, blinking into the morning light with sleep-sensitive eyes. There, in the doorway, stood an enormous man—at least six-five—in an anonymous black suit and black tie. He was wearing sunglasses and was rather good-looking in a somewhat frightening, FBI-agent sort of way.

"Twenty-eight?"

Monique blinked.

"Uh—yes?"

The man held out a card. Monique saw that it was Pietre's card.

"My name is James. I've been instructed to bring you to Mr. Salazar."

Monique felt an intense wave of emotions. Was she being summoned so that she could be punished? Or was this to be her next training session?

Best to play it cool.

"All right," she said, smiling. "Just let me put on some clothes."

"No clothes," said the man without emotion. "I've been instructed to bring you as you are."

Monique's eyes went wide. "But—you've got to let me put on some clothes."

"I have my instructions," said the man. "I suggest you don't attempt to disobey me."

Monique felt a warmth flooding into her lower body as she heard the big, powerful guy say that. He was an agent of Pietre's, and Monique felt as intense a desire to obey him as she felt to obey Alfred or Pietre.

"Well—all right," said Monique. "May I at least brush my teeth? Put on some shoes?"

"No," said the man. "And don't bring your house keys, either."

The man's black limousine was parked in front of the house. It had frightened Monique intensely to walk out of the house wearing nothing but that skimpy, lacy black satin robe she'd purchased at Next to Nothing. It was early enough on a Sunday that there wasn't really anyone on the streets of the faceless, anonymous suburb. So there was no one to see Monique as she darted from the house to the limousine. The man closed the door behind her, and Monique felt an intense excitement as she realized that she'd just been locked out of the house. Without her keys, she was completely and totally at this man's mercy. At Pietre's mercy.

The windows of the limousine were mirrored, so the people in the streets couldn't see Monique's state of undress as they drove past them. To her surprise, she felt her nipples hardening as they passed a crowd of people mingling outside a church. Monique slowly pulled open the little robe, exposing her breasts with their firm pink buds, savoring the feeling that the churchgoers couldn't see her. She began to touch her breasts, pinch her nipples, tease herself.

She'd been ordered by Alfred to masturbate—just not to orgasm. So she was obeying his commands by doing this.

Loving the sensation of being nude before all these churchgoers, Monique leaned back on the plush seats of the limousine and opened the robe all the way. She toyed with her aching, overwrought pussy as, outside, folks prepared to enter their own house of worship.

Soon Monique was dripping wet and panting, anticipating the training she was about to receive.

She was forced to stop her self-pleasuring when the limousine pulled up into the turnaround of Pietre's mansion. James came around and opened the passenger door.

Monique quickly pulled the skimpy robe shut, and tied it. She got out of the limousine, loving the knowledge that she was almost naked, but protected by the high fences and shrubs that shrouded Pietre's mansion. The Master did love his privacy.

Inside the house, Monique was led by James down a long hallway she hadn't seen before. Like the other halls in the house, it was lined with antique paintings of nude or semi-nude women in poses of either erotic splendor or some sort of subtle submission. An art critic might not have noticed the submissive poses of the women—but Monique could *only* notice, her nipples and sex throbbing as she passed frame after frame of women on their knees or sprawled, exposed and vulnerable, naked and helpless.

Soon they were going through a door and into a dank, cold-smelling darkness, down a spiral staircase. *I'm being taken into the basement,* thought Monique, her sex tingling at the prospect. *Maybe this is where the dungeon is. The dungeon.* Monique turned the word over and over again in her head. *Am I to be punished?*

Monique felt a surge of desire as she imagined her nude body, spread open for all of Pietre's punishments.

Sure enough, Monique was led into a large, dark room with candles burning in sconces on the walls. She felt her body responding with sexual arousal, despite the ache in her sex from overuse. Monique was so powerfully aroused by the thought of being taken in Pietre's dungeon that she almost stumbled as she looked around.

The lighting was not very good, so Monique could only see the shadows of the equipment that was going to be used to torment her. She thought she saw whips on the walls, but she couldn't be sure. Perhaps she glimpsed clamps, paddles, canes. She couldn't be sure, in the shadows.

"Remove your robe," ordered James, and Monique obeyed, standing naked in the flickering light.

James guided Monique up to a wall that was fitted with an elaborate system of manacles. She felt her pussy juicing as the man's strong, powerful arms forced her into the shackles. First she was made to stand in the right place; her wrists were fitted into a set of manacles above her head. Monique felt herself creaming at the feeling of being restrained like this. Then James bent down and forced Monique's ankles into similar shackles. As he closed the cold circles of metal around Monique's ankles, she whimpered in pleasure.

Then a thick leather belt was fitted around Monique's waist, to hold her body in place. She squirmed a little to test her bonds, becoming intensely aroused as she realized that she was completely and totally restrained.

Finally, a metal shackle closed around her neck. Monique could feel the cold of the steel locking her in place, forcing her to hold her head up.

Then several more pieces folded out, as James locked them around Monique's head. She felt a padded cup being pressed onto her chin, then locking so that her head was held immobile. To force her to remain even more rigidly immobile, there were two padded bars which folded down on either side of her head.

Now she couldn't move at all—not to turn her head, look up or down. Not to writhe or squirm or try to get away.

She was totally, completely, restrained. Entirely helpless. Naked and revealed before this strangely attractive man, this stranger. A complete stranger who could explore Monique's vulnerable body all he wanted... without her being able to stop him.

A surge went through Monique's sex. She fancied that she could feel her sex dribbling juice on the floor between her wide-open legs.

James went around and blew out each one of the candles, until the dungeon was in total darkness. Then James vanished into the darkness; Monique heard his footsteps as he walked away.

With her head held rigidly in this position, she wouldn't have been able to see much of anything even if the candles had still been burning.

Monique's body was reacting with powerful sexual desire to the sensation of being restrained like this. And the fear that she was about to be punished.

Would Pietre punish Monique by refusing to fuck her?

Monique's sex lubricated still more as she wondered if that good-looking, powerful driver had wanted to fuck her. Of course he had. He had had a very naked and vulnerable Monique pressed against him as he shackled her to the wall. Of course he must have felt a desire to fuck her. Monique wondered if he had gotten hard—she hadn't been able to tell from the way he'd been holding her body. Monique felt her mind running away with her, bringing more tingling sensations and pulses of desire to her naked, immobilized body. Maybe James had a dick that was in proportion to his body. And maybe, instead of shackling Monique to the wall, he wanted to tie her to the floor, spread out for him, then to mount the helpless Monique and press his enormous cock inside her, taking her virginity as she moaned and writhed, begging for more of his huge cock—

Monique gasped as blinding lights suddenly went on—three of them, so bright that Monique moaned in pain as the light tore into her eyes. She couldn't see a thing—could only feel the pain as the bright light filled he consciousness. Even shutting her eyes tightly didn't help. She couldn't turn her head even a little bit—she was restrained by the metal shackle around her neck and the pieces holding her face. She was forced to look directly at the light, and closing her eyes only seemed to make the light redder, as her blood vessels throbbed in pain.

"You have disobeyed us, Twenty-eight?"

It was Alfred's voice, over some sort of amplifier.

Monique felt a wave of nausea, an overwhelming feeling of regret. She whimpered. The light was exposing all her sordid secrets.

"Well, Twenty-eight? What have you done to disobey us?"

Monique didn't know why she did it, but she suddenly decided to come clean. She would expose everything, confess every transgression. Beg for mercy.

"I—I tried not to disobey you," she moaned. "I'm sorry."

"You pleasured yourself?" came Alfred's amplified
voice.

"Yes, yes," gasped Monique. "But I didn't make myself
come."

"Excellent," Alfred said. "How many times did you
pleasure yourself without coming?"

"I don't remember," moaned Monique desperately.

"You must remember." It was a new voice, harsh and
unforgiving—a woman's voice. But whose? Monique
didn't recognize it.

Monique's mind, overloaded with fear and remorse,
searched desperately for the information. There had
been the time on the couch, then at the pool, then on
the couch, then on the deck, the shower, in bed, on her
parents bed—

"I—I don't remember," she wailed.

"You do remember."

"A—A dozen, at least. At least. Two dozen, perhaps.
Maybe more. I—I lost count."

"When did you lose count?" came Pietre's voice.

"At—at twelve or so. Maybe ten. I lost count! I'm so
sorry—I just couldn't help myself!"

"And so you did not climax at all since last you were
in this house?"

"No," Monique said, her voice taking on a slightly surly tone as she felt the ache in her pussy and stomach that told her she desperately needed to come.

"But you've transgressed in other ways, certainly."

"I...I don't know," said Monique nervously.

"I'm sure you did transgress. Surely you've been displaying yourself shamelessly to men and women. As you were instructed to do. But you've gone too far, haven't you?"

"Yes," gasped Monique, remembering- how good it had felt to feel Chelsea rub her clit till she came. Knowing that that little shrew Chelsea had probably told Pietre and Alfred everything.

She had transgressed.

"Tell us of your transgression," came Alfred's voice. "Offer us every detail."

"Leave nothing out," Pietre's voice added, with a tone of zest and relish.

Monique searched her mind for the details. She would have to tell them everything....

"I—it started in the park," she began.

CHAPTER 15

Monique confessed every detail of her long Saturday of debauched pleasure. She told her new Masters the whole story of her disobedience and near-disobedience.

How she had all but begged Brianna to make love to her, displaying her body brazenly to her. How she had shamelessly teased Chelsea. Begged Chelsea with her body and her eyes and her lips to touch her pussy and make her come. And how Chelsea had done just that. How she had kissed Miss Trustmore at Bonne Femme. How Cassidy at Chained Heat had spanked her.

Monique told everything. Every tiny detail of her sexual actions over the last twenty-four hours and just before. Surely she had rarely actually crossed the boundaries, but she told them the details anyway—letting them know how frequently she had thought about transgressing. How frequently she had thought about disobeying her Master.

Thought about coming. Thought about being fucked.

Every confession she made sent a new flood of pleasure into her naked body as she described all the things she had done. Soon Monique was dripping on the floor, her hard nipples throbbing with excitement. It was torture to be made to confess like this without being able to satisfy herself.

When she finally finished, she was panting and exhausted in her shackles, her muscles and joints aching, her sex dripping, and her bodily need overwhelming her.

"Please," she begged, wishing they would punish her by driving their cocks into her. Punishing her with ecstasy. What she needed. "Please forgive me."

Monique was taken down from the shackles by James. The lights were dimmed slightly, and Monique was lowered onto a padded table. Dimly, Monique felt her wrists being bound over her head. Then she felt her legs being lifted, placed in a spread-wide position.

She felt padded cuffs being buckled around her ankles, too. She moaned softly, thinking of Chelsea's pierced pussy. Was she to be pierced, as well?

When Monique felt her clit being teased, she knew the worst was true. And yet, the idea of being marked like this brought a surge of heat to her pussy. She moaned softly as she felt her clit being teased into a metal clamp.

Monique let out a gasp of pain as the clamp was drawn tight.

"Breathe," came a familiar voice—very familiar. "Breath. Like this." There were the sounds of rhythmic breathing and Monique tried to duplicate them.

Then there was the feeling of a mouth against hers, kissing her hard, tongue teasing her lips apart as Monique felt the searing pain through her clit. Agony filled her whole body as she tried to assimilate the pain, the new piece of metal being forced through her clit.

"Breathe," came the familiar voice again, and Chelsea looked at Monique, smiling wickedly from between her legs. She wore rubber gloves and held a needle in her hand. A needle slick with Monique's blood.

"Just the clit, for now," sighed Chelsea. "You haven't proven yourself to be the slut that I did. But soon, maybe." Then Chelsea giggled.

Monique tried to look down and see what had been done to her. But she couldn't quite move. She could feel hands on her breasts, teasing her nipples.

"I really think we should pierce these," came another familiar voice, closer to Monique's ear. Try as she might, Monique could not place it. "She deserves it, you know. Always flashing them shamelessly."

"My dear, that is exactly the point," came Alfred's voice. "She should be showing them off. As should you."

There was a stony silence.

"Yes, Master," came Miss Pynchon's voice, and she kissed Monique on the forehead. "Little slut," she growled under her breath.

Monique tried again to lift her head, to see what havoc had been wreaked upon her clit. The pain had begun to diminish, but she still felt a strong ache in there. There was a sting as she felt Chelsea cleaning her off.

"Would you like a mirror?" asked Chelsea. "To see what we've done to you?" she giggled.

Monique nodded, and Chelsea held up a small mirror. The only light in the room was focused clearly on Monique's lower half, and Monique could see her new ring quite clearly. There was something disturbingly beautiful about the way her shaved pussy looked with that ring at its top. The ring went through her clit vertically, a bright steel ornament with a shimmering jewel of red.

"It's a ruby," said Chelsea. "I only got an amethyst. But then, I guess he had to give me a lot more rings." Her lascivious wink was followed by another laugh out of the darkness.

"Same here." Cassidy? Monique couldn't tell.

Then, unmistakably, Brianna's voice. "We'll have this slut whoring around in no time, begging for a ring in every part of her body. She'll have to wear a harness day-in and day-out before we're done."

"Brianna, this is no laughing matter. You're next, after Chelsea. Now, Chelsea? It's your turn." It was Pietre's voice, out of the darkness. Monique could see Chelsea turning quickly beet-red.

"Yes, Master," she said saucily.

Chelsea was wearing a tight, somewhat tacky retro-Seventies orange tube top and a pink plastic skirt. She took off the tube top and then moved to the skirt, which she unzipped and let fall to the floor. Then she bent over the edge of the table to which Monique was strapped. This put Chelsea's face just a few inches from Monique's pussy and her freshly-pierced clit.

"So near and yet so far," sighed Chelsea.

Then Monique saw, dimly, the unmistakable figure of Pietre, clad head-to-toe in leather.

He was holding a long, flexible implement. Monique shivered.

There was a loud *swish*, and Chelsea's whole body jerked. She whimpered and gasped.

"I'm sorry, Master," she moaned softly.

"I know you are," growled Pietre. "Bitch!" The switch came down again, and Chelsea spasmed in pain. She groaned.

Another blow. Chelsea's hot breath was on Monique's bare pussy as she gasped and panted. Another. Chelsea let out a wail of agony.

"Spread your legs wider," ordered Pietre.

"No, master," pleaded Chelsea desperately. But there was a tone of excitement to her voice, as if she was so aroused she was about to explode. "Please, not there!"

"Open them! Slut!"

Obediently, whimpering as though she was on the verge of tears, Chelsea snuggled her body down against the table and opened her legs wider.

Then the switch came down, and Chelsea's wails almost became screams.

"Sorry, Master," she gasped. "Sorry, sorry, sorry!"

"Yes, you are," said Pietre. "Cassidy, place the harness on her."

"Yes, Master," said Cassidy. So the whole day had been a calculated exercise to test Monique's resolve. And now, since she'd failed, she had been pierced.

But Chelsea had failed more profoundly, it seemed, that Monique. *At least I haven't been whipped*—yet, Monique thought to herself as Cassidy came around behind Chelsea.

Chelsea was weeping softly, her tears splashing warm onto Monique's pussy. Monique hated to admit to herself that there was something intensely erotic about that.

It was hard for Monique to see what Cassidy was doing to Chelsea. But when Cassidy positioned herself behind Chelsea's pert exposed ass, Chelsea let out a gasp and then a low moan.

"All the way in," said Cassidy soothingly. "Come on, open up."

"No, no, Master, it's too big," groaned Chelsea.

"It is not," said Cassidy with a tone of scolding. "Open up."

Chelsea's nude body shuddered, and she grasped at Monique's legs with her hands. Monique could still feel Chelsea's tears falling on her pussy.

Chelsea let out a sudden sigh of relief.

"Good," said Cassidy. "Now the other."

"Oh, God, no, no, no, no, please..." Chelsea moaned.

"Come on, you've proven you need it!"

Then Chelsea was choking, sobbing, gasping with exertion as Cassidy worked on her. Chelsea reverently kissed Monique's inner thighs.

"I wish I was like you," she gasped. "Lucy little virgin —oh! Oh, God!"

"There," said Cassidy. "All the way in. That wasn't really *all* that big, was it?"

"Yes," growled Chelsea. "It was."

"Well, you brought it on yourself," said Cassidy unsympathetically. "Now just let me buckle you in."

"Normally he wouldn't fill both holes for a transgression like this," said Miss Pynchon softly as she stroked Monique's brow. "But Chelsea's such a slut. She's proven it over and over again. And it wasn't just you she fucked yesterday."

"Now you've one hole left open," said Pietre sternly.

273

"Do I have to send you back to work wearing a gag? Perhaps one in the shape of the dick you so dearly love?"

"No," said Chelsea miserably. "I will obey, Master."

"Good, you slut. Then get over here and show me what you did to that rotten boyfriend of yours."

Chelsea didn't need to be asked twice. She eagerly left Monique's table and dropped to her knees before Pietre.

Monique strained to get a look, but couldn't see Pietre well enough in the dark room. She could see Chelsea's blonde pigtails flashing from time to time.

"I've got a better angle," whispered Miss Pynchon. "I'll tell you what I see...that little slut down on her knees. She's got his pants open. She's sucking it down. All the way, in one gulp. Mr. Salazar is so well-hung, dear. It's really quite impressive that she can do that. She's got it all down into her throat. Now she's working him up and down. Mmmm, she's really so delicious —he should do this to her more often. I guess knowing she can't be fucked makes her hungry for more cock in her mouth. Do you think that's true of you, dear?"

Monique moaned softly.

Miss Pynchon kissed her tenderly.

"She's picking up speed," said Miss Pynchon. "He must be getting close. Oh yes. He's going to come. There! My, she's not getting it all, is she? All over her breasts. But she seems not to mind that.

"Oh! Alfred's next, of course. My, she's giving him an even more royal treatment. Using those breasts of hers, now that they're all slick with the Master's come. Do you think you would like that, Monique? If the Master were to slide his cock right between these lovely breasts of yours? I mean, Chelsea's got such ripe ones —but yours are even bigger! Oh—there he goes! Right onto her—she barely caught any of it in her mouth. Some girls are like that, you know. Don't like to swallow, so they want it all over them. Do you think you would be like that, Monique? Or would you like to swallow it?"

Monique squirmed desperately, the agony in her clit growing as she felt it getting more and more erect and pumped with blood.

"Goodness, you're bleeding—just a little—nothing serious. Cassidy? Could you see to this?"

"Right away, Brooke." Cassidy obediently rubbed Monique's clit with an antiseptic wipe. Monique moaned softly.

Monique looked up at Miss Pynchon as Alfred addressed them all.

"All right," he said. "You all have your instructions. James will drive you each home."

Monique rode home in the limousine with Cassidy, Miss Pynchon—Brooke?—Brianna, and the chastised Chelsea. Kendra and Kelly—whom Monique knew as

Miss Trustmore—had been lurking in the shadows as well, observing the punishment while bound to the wall. Monique didn't ask about those details.

Monique was fascinated by the sensations in her newly pierced clit. And even though the limousine looked big on the outside, it felt so crowded in here —with all these girls all over her. Monique was already getting turned on, which only brought an ache—a real ache—to her swollen clit.

Miss Pynchon was not dressed at all as Monique was used to. Rather, her skirt was at least eight inches above the knee. She still wore her horn-rimmed glasses, but with her hair down like that they looked somehow naughty. Monique couldn't help looking at the low-cut blouse which did little to hide the shape of Miss Pynchon's breasts. She had never seen this woman looking so delicious.

Monique wanted to undress her.

No, she had to stop thinking like that! She was going to be severely punished if she kept disobeying Pietre and Alfred! She had to take her mind off her pulsing sex.

But it wasn't easy in that car full of slave-girls, all of whom served the same master. And each of whom Monique desperately wanted to touch.

Chelsea, who had put her pink plastic mini-skirt back on, was sitting with quite obvious discomfort. She shifted nervously, moaning every now and then when the limousine hit a bump in the road—despite the striking smoothness of the ride.

Monique wondered if she would be given the same treatment some day.

The limousine slowly emptied out as James dropped off the girls at work—all except Monique and Miss Pynchon. First Kendra and Cassidy were let off at Chained Heat. Then Chelsea and Brianna were dropped off at the mall.

That left Monique and Miss Pynchon. James pulled up in front of Monique's house.

She lingered at the window as Miss Pynchon held her hand.

Monique could feel the tangible bond of submission between them, even while she knew that it was her place to submit to Miss Pynchon. Clearly there was a power structure involved, and Miss Pynchon, while no doubt deeply submissive to Pietre, still commanded Monique's unflinching obedience.

That thought sent a quiver through Monique's sex.

She looked into Miss Pynchon's eyes.

"Thank you, Miss Pynchon," she sighed.

Miss Pynchon chuckled cruelly, then giggled in a shockingly girlish manner.

"Call me Brooke," she said cheerfully, and got out of the car.